MW01131431

Coven Master

Paranormal Huntress Series, Volume 2

W.J. May

Published by Dark Shadow Publishing, 2017.

This is a work of fiction. Similarities to real people, places, or events are entirely coincidental.

COVEN MASTER

First edition. August 30, 2017.

Copyright © 2017 W.J. May.

Written by W.J. May.

Also by W.J. May

Bit-Lit Series
Lost Vampire
Cost of Blood
Price of Death

Blood Red Series
Courage Runs Red
The Night Watch
Marked by Courage
Forever Night

Daughters of Darkness: Victoria's Journey
Victoria
Huntress
Coveted (A Vampire & Paranormal Romance)
Twisted

Hidden Secrets Saga

Seventh Mark - Part 1
Seventh Mark - Part 2
Marked By Destiny
Compelled
Fate's Intervention
Chosen Three
The Hidden Secrets Saga: The Complete Series

Paranormal Huntress Series
Never Look Back
Coven Master

Prophecy Series
Only the Beginning
White Winter
Secrets of Destiny

The Chronicles of Kerrigan
Rae of Hope
Dark Nebula
House of Cards
Royal Tea
Under Fire
End in Sight
Hidden Darkness
Twisted Together
Mark of Fate
Strength & Power

Last One Standing
Rae of Light
The Chronicles of Kerrigan Box Set Books # 1 - 6

The Chronicles of Kerrigan: Gabriel
Living in the Past
Present For Today

The Chronicles of Kerrigan Prequel
Christmas Before the Magic
Question the Darkness
Into the Darkness
Fight the Darkness
Alone in the Darkness
Lost in Darkness
The Chronicles of Kerrigan Prequel Series Books #1-3

The Chronicles of Kerrigan Sequel
A Matter of Time
Time Piece
Second Chance
Glitch in Time
Our Time
Precious Time

The Hidden Secrets Saga

Seventh Mark (part 1 & 2)

The Senseless Series
Radium Halos
Radium Halos - Part 2
Nonsense

Standalone
Shadow of Doubt (Part 1 & 2)
Five Shades of Fantasy
Shadow of Doubt - Part 2
Four and a Half Shades of Fantasy
Dream Fighter
What Creeps in the Night
Forest of the Forbidden
HuNted
Arcane Forest: A Fantasy Anthology
Ancient Blood of the Vampire and Werewolf

Paranormal Huntress Series #2

Coven Master

By W.J. May

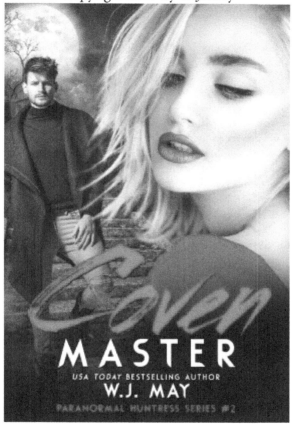

Paranormal Huntress Series

Find W.J. May

Website:
http://www.wanitamay.yolasite.com
Facebook:
https://www.facebook.com/pages/Author-WJ-May-FAN-PAGE/141170442608149
Newsletter:
SIGN UP FOR W.J. May's Newsletter to find out about new releases, updates, cover reveals and FREE READS!
http://eepurl.com/97aYf

Coven Master Blurb

The wise learn many things from their enemies.

The city of Calen has fallen.

The forces that once held the city as one are scattered and drained of power. Adelaide, one of the witches who has haunted and threatened the peace once made by the elders in the territory, has regained her power by releasing the hybrids she's created. She's determined to destroy Calen and all those who stand in her way.

Atlanta, the Druid huntress, responsible for unlocking the hybrids and the murder of her uncle, tries to come to terms with what's happened. Determined to try to set the wrong right she enlists the help of her kind, willing to risk everything, including her life, to stop Adelaide.

Suddenly she finds herself in a different town, fighting the witch and facing secrets about her past that leave her overwhelmed and vulnerable.

Meanwhile, Ryan and Marcus are in Calen, uncertain of what's happened to Atlanta and desperate to find her. They must face the hybrids over and over as the waves of power press down on them.

The fate of Calen rests in too few hands. Divided sanctions, Vamps, Wolf, and Druid, must unify—or each race stands no chance of survival.

Chapter 1

A blaze of velvet red pierced the fine white sky. Silhouettes of birds and echoes of their morning song resounded in the air. They soared high, as if escaping some sullen malice that lay underneath. They formed an array of poetic welcoming for the rising of the sun in the broad and warm skies of the city of Lisbon.

The waves surrendered to the magnetic call of the shore's lips. The mountains behind spoke in silence as they were swallowed by grey skies. At the base of the mountains, on the other side from the shore, a slim figure strolled through the rocky steeps. His movement so silent that, even within the stillness that surrounded him, the echo of his footsteps was a mere whisper.

He walked with purpose, eyes set on a destination in front of him, unblinking as the winds curled and tossed around him.

The rocks on the mountain ahead of him were in shades of dark grey and reddish brown. He gazed at them for a moment from afar, then turned his head to a nearly twenty-foot-tall yellow rock formation to his right. He approached the rocks while constantly scanning his surroundings, making sure he wasn't being followed. He listened for the sound of footsteps or even the tremble of stones nearby. Nothing could be missed.

Satisfied that he was indeed alone, he knelt before the limestone rocks and reached out to a dirty greenish rock that sat alone, engulfed within the yellowness of the rocks. He pushed the rock into the wall. In seconds, a passageway right behind the rock formation was revealed and he became swallowed inside it.

Surrounded by darkness he swiftly made his way down the narrow passageways, deeper into the mountain.

It didn't take him long to reach the end of his trek. He pressed his hand against a glass door and waited patiently until it slid open. Instantly bathed in fluorescent lights that shone whiter than snow, he blinked and let his eyes adjust. He walked in, through the tunnel of light, and down a second passageway much clearer than the first. His footsteps echoed as he picked up speed. His high black boots rang with the sounds of metal chains.

It was like a maze of tunnels bathed in brightness. He opened doors, turned left and right, and almost robotically moved toward a destination known only to him. The force with which he pushed the doors open gave the impression that the thin man was either quite angry or agitated. The shades of red on his forehead and the sweat running down his cheeks were both a sign of distress and the product of the endless walking he had to endure.

But even though his breathing was heavy and labored, he didn't stop to rest. For nearly thirty minutes he roamed the tunnels, pushing through one door after the other, driven by instinct and an obscure purpose known only to him.

He finally stopped at a hallway with three doors. He fixed his gaze on the one right across from him, marched towards it, then hesitated.

Wrong one.

He turned and pushed the bar on the door to his left and swiftly slipped inside.

There were mirrors on every wall and on the ceiling. The floor was adorned with a plush, bright-red rug. The room was hexagonal in shape and the lights inside burned a bluish white that made his eyes water.

The floor and the bars that hung on every corner looked like those in the basement of the Skolars back in Calen.

The man finally took a moment to stop and catch his breath before walking towards the small brown door in between two mirrors.

He pressed his finger on a small round button to the right and waited. "It's Raul," he said.

Seconds later a buzzer sounded and the lock on the door released. Raul pushed the door open into a room similar to the one he'd just left. But, unlike the mirrors on every wall, this one gleamed with portraits and paintings in golden frames. Each painting depicted a man or a woman in crimson red or dark blue suit. The paintings were engraved with dates that went back centuries.

A round table in the middle of the room caught Raul's attention. Four people sat, two on each side, their attention drawn to a fifth man standing on his own. The conversations had stopped as everyone turned to look at the newcomer.

"Raul?"

Raul looked at the young man in charge of the meeting and swiftly made his way to him. "Sorry for interrupting," he said, the urgency in his voice grabbing everyone's attention. "I know it isn't my place, but I have some terribly important news."

Not that entering a hidden building and barging into a secret meeting wasn't important.

This, however, couldn't wait.

Raul didn't wait for a response. "It's about the city of Calen."

Chapter 2

Calen

Midnight was a glimpse away; the hours passed as if minutes were dust that flew out of a broken hourglass. There were desolate shafts of light that would peek into the streets, trying hard to shed themselves over the darkened corners of the city, all in vain. The dust filled the air, casting its shadow over the towers of Calen. If one would gaze at the city from afar, they'd think that a sandstorm had caught the pillars of every building with its rough claws.

Along with the darkness, there wasn't a single moment of silence. Not a second passed without the heavy sound of cracking, or confused screams, or the zapping of wires ripped out of their circuits. The city itself was crumbling, along with the people inside it.

In the suburbs, the Skolar house sat in ruins. Shingles were strewn about on either side of the house, and the grass looked as if it was reaching out to swallow the crushed skeleton of what remained of the house. Half the grass had yellowed from lack of sun, but oddly continued to grow. The other half had been scorched. Only the basement was the only part that laid untouched, unharmed by the constant hail of fire that fell from the gargoyles' breath onto the streets of Calen.

Further into the city, the majestic gothic structure of Calen High stood proud. Oddly, with minor damage done to it. As Adelaide's hybrids roamed the dust ridden corners of the city, Marcus waited inside.

We're all doomed.

Marcus stepped out of the principal's office, where he had spent the past few days regaining his strength. He stretched, letting his fangs elongate and retract, as if making sure they would still obey his will. He gazed down the dark, empty hallways, wondering how this could have happened.

It'd been nearly two weeks since the door had been opened.

By the end of the first day, it was no secret the hybrids were out. Adelaide made sure everyone—mortal or supernatural—knew her forces were taking over the city. Marcus remembered it clearly, as if it had happened just yesterday. He'd been in his thirteenth-floor office, surrounded by the best of his guards, when the heavy roaring of the wind first began to howl through the city. It was followed by the sound of shattering windows and the fusion of metals bombarding into one another.

Marcus had stepped out onto the terrace of his office, surrounded by a thick blanket of dust and wind that prevented him from seeing anything further than a few feet away. He had felt the grains scrape against his skin and eyes, threatening to engulf him, making sure Adelaide's hybrids could operate under its shroud unhindered.

He knew he could not be compelled by the hybrids, knew that the elders of the Vampire clan were immune to the beasts' trickery. Still, there was little they could do when they couldn't see, or sense, the enemy.

Adelaide had clearly been counting on that.

She's bloody planned every step. Been planning for years.

The memory still burned in the back of his mind. How he'd walked back into his office to find his guards dead. How the wind had howled all around him and red eyes had peeked through the clouds of dust surrounding him. They'd come for him, three of the beasts, eager to rid themselves of the threat Marcus posed to their dominance. They were a formidable force, but he had no intention of letting them win. In the end, he'd gotten the better of them. He could still feel their green hearts pounding in his palm before he crushed them.

If only we could've controlled them.

Marcus barked in laughter and shook his head. Even now, alone and without a plan, he was thinking of how he could use this attack to his advantage. The desire to be the dominant race, to be king of all, was etched in his every bone, and the fact that he was now prey to something even more superior bothered him tremendously.

The Druids. I need to find the Druids.

But even that idea seemed senseless. James was the last Druid, and he hadn't seen the man since the nightmare had started. Atlanta was missing, too. Marcus knew James was dead, but Atlanta... what had happened to her?

Not that I would know. I've been locked up in here for a fortnight.

Even though the hybrids had fallen, he had taken quite a beating. It had taken all his strength to storm out of the lair and find his way here, to hide in the shadows and regain his strength. His healing had taken time, more time than he was used to, and he knew it was because of the poison that coursed through Adelaide's hybrids.

He'd been frozen by her charms before.

An anger burned deep inside him as he walked down the empty corridors of Calen High. Every few steps, his eyes would catch the decaying corpse of a fallen human. He had fed on the ones still alive when he'd arrived.

Students torn to shreds, teachers gasping blood. They were going to die anyway, and he'd needed all the blood he could get to recover. Now their corpses looked like mangled pieces of flesh, the rot they emitted burning his sinuses.

We need to regroup.

Marcus scoffed at the thought. Regroup where? And how? He didn't even know if there was anyone alive who could fight alongside him. He knew he couldn't trust anyone other than the elders of his own group, yet he doubted even their survival. He was going to have to find out either way. They would need everyone able to fight against Adelaide and the hybrids.

Inside the nearly unmoving corridors, the whistling sound of water running down the broken dispensers barely muffled the screaming outside. The costume of the school mascot lay on the floor of the hallway, torn to pieces. Marcus walked on the ceramic floors that were tiled in blue and red squares, between open lockers with their hinges scattered around the floor. Pages torn from books were dust-ridden and flying about. He made his way to the back exit of the school.

It was nearly dusk outside, the crickets barely whispering as the football goalposts turned a pale shade of yellow. Marcus sprinted towards the posts, one after the other, testing his strength and making sure he was fully recovered before he could venture beyond the protection of Calen High.

I need to find the others.

Even though his centuries'-old pride whispered at the back of his mind that he alone could take down an empire of hybrids, he remembered he was also the reason this was happening. It was his blood that gave birth to the malice that encompassed the city.

It might not be directly, but he was responsible for everything.

He couldn't shake the thought that, without the Druids, they couldn't have stood a chance against the hybrids a century before. He remembered how the Werewolves had fought alongside the Druids in the insurgence, a massive force he'd marveled at. Back then, it had seemed like the Vampires were actually holding everyone down. Marcus scowled at the memory. They'd been so helpless back then.

As they were helpless now.

The level of humiliation Adelaide had thrown upon his race enraged him.

Never again.

He leapt from the tall football bleachers, frowning as his eyes glowed a bloody shade of red. His movements were swift as he dashed across the field and left the temporary haven of Calen High. He roamed every street and every rooftop of every tower in Calen. And as his feet pounded the concrete of the streets, his eyes could still see his own Vampires glaring at him as he ran. Some tried to reach for him, and he slashed through them as if they were paper, ripping them apart with a sickening ease he took no comfort in.

They're not mine anymore. They're compelled.

Marcus searched many places before finally reaching the three towers where James Skolar had been. The dust seemed less dense here, and the green of the forests behind him glowed in the morning sun. His eyes were met by the flickering of red light on top of one of the roofs, a little underneath from where the sun was shining.

He dashed into the building, and within seconds found himself crashing through the rooftop door. His feet crunched on the pebble-covered floor, his eyes catching sight of the destruction across the neighboring towers.

There's been a fight here.

The ground to his right had been carved with a body that was missing, and his keen eyesight caught droplets of caked blood on the pebbles around. There were stains of blood at the right corner of the roof, and he caught a whiff of something pungent, something dark.

From the corner of his eye, he caught movement.

Marcus turned quickly, immediately ready for a fight, fangs stretched and craving to sink themselves in flesh. A few yards away his eyes fell on a body, motionless except for the rise and fall of labored breathing.

Marcus relaxed, retracting his fangs as the harsh reality sunk in.

Ryan Toller.

Chapter 3

Darian's presence always demanded respect.

As the leader of The Coven, one could not deny the power that seemed to ooze from him wherever he went. His slightly broad shoulders and piercing pale-blue eyes demanded attention, and always seemed attentive and assertive. His light-brown hair was sparse on the sides and stood up on the top of his head. His sideburns reached just under his earlobes; his beard a mere shade over his angular cheekbones. He was young, but the knowledge he possessed was well beyond his years.

Before Raul had come in, Darian had gathered the eldest of the Druids in his region to discuss their interference with the conflict that had been raging in a small town in Armenia. The Vampires in the surrounding area had decided to assert their dominance and attacked, wiping out the entire town.

Darian, obviously distressed over the issue, felt a need to send some of the Druids over to investigate and resolve the problem. And, if necessary, remain there to protect the town. The leaders he was meeting with were mostly in agreement with everything he was suggesting. However, they were reluctant to go there themselves and the matter was too small to require all of them to attend to it.

Except Darian felt it a responsibility of his own to take even the most extreme measures to make sure the Vampires weren't harming, let alone killing people The Coven was meant to be protecting. He made it a point to use instances like this to make an example of those who fell out of line. It wasn't because of the responsibility of being the leader, which was to ensure the safety of the people, but more the nature of who Darian was. The combination of duty and the guilt had been passed down through the centuries, generation to generation, until it ran in his blood.

Although only twenty, what he lacked in experience he made up for in knowledge that could be sensed from merely looking in his eyes. Darian's wisdom exceeded that of men twice his age. The man knew how to think things through, and his insight to the others was never challenged—often—anymore. His young intelligence was incomprehensible to many.

When Raul walked in, Darian immediately noticed the drop of sweat sitting on the man's forehead. He could hear his friend's heavy breathing disguised in the controlled slow pace that Raul tried to maintain.

"Lost in the labyrinth again?" Darian asked, addressing his friend in a confident and comforting tone.

"My memory of those doors is rusty," Raul replied.

"Well, welcome back, friend!" Darian said, pointing to the chair across from him, signaling for Raul to sit down.

Raul gazed at the others and then back at Darian, his lips stretched in a slight smile. "Happy I'm back?"

"Your disappearance made me fear the worst," Darian responded.

"I'm still around." Raul smiled, but Darian didn't miss the exhaustion in his friend's eyes. "It was impossible... even miles around Calen, there was no way I could reach here. Our signals have been jammed."

Darian wasn't surprised. "All right, gentlemen, shall we continue this meeting another time? I'd like a private word with Raul, here."

The leaders left with displeased looks on their faces. It was no secret they despised the fact that a man much younger than they, for some even half their age, was calling and dismissing them, ordering and disordering them whenever he wanted. However, they knew better than to act on their discontent. Darian knew that. They all recognized the power he possessed, and knew that, because he was the descendant of the former Coven, he was the only one fit to lead them.

They left the room with Darian sitting across Raul. The formality dissipated the moment the door was closed and the friendship between the two showed. Darian got up and walked over to one of the paintings on his left, then slid it down from its frame. There was the classic safe behind the painting; however, this one didn't hide any gold, but a bottle of wine and glasses.

He brought the wine and sat closer to Raul. "A drink to celebrate your return, my friend."

"After what I've just seen, one bottle isn't going to be enough," Raul replied, his words followed with a sigh as he wiped the sweat off his forehead with the sleeve of his shirt.

Months before Darian had given Raul, a junior Druid, the task of tracking down the settlers in the west and mainly in America, to try to find out where the concentration of Vampires and Werewolves had settled. Raul had communicated with Darian many times during the long months of his journey. However, upon reaching Calen, all communication had been lost.

The elders who had sat around the table had never heard of the city of Calen. The despair in Raul's voice seemed unnecessary to all of them because the city was foreign. However, Darian knew Raul had come back to confirm what had troubled Darian's mind for years.

Darian was known to be a very patient man. Even after seeing the distress on Raul's face, he didn't ask for the news immediately. Rather, the two drank the wine and talked endlessly until Raul's face softened and the harshness eased. Darian didn't need to hear Raul's story before attempting to find a solution. Rather, every small expression on Raul's face was a sentence that spoke to him on its own, and in response Darian had already begun planning his next step. As Raul was rambled on, Darian's mind began working in a completely different direction.

"All right, friend, it's time," Darian said. Raul immediately straightened in his seat and pushed his empty glass away. "What happen in Calen?" Darian asked.

"Do you know James Skolar?" Raul replied.

"I've heard of the Skolars. They were the leaders of the American Druids a long time ago. What about him?"

"I found him when I reached Calen or, more specifically, he found me. Apparently, his is—was—the only remaining family of Druids there, and for the past century they've managed to live in complete harmony with both the Vampires and Werewolves."

"You said *was* the only family." Darian noted the look on Raul's face, and didn't like it. Something wasn't right.

"That's why I came rushing back," replied Raul. "James Skolar is dead. His niece, the only remaining Druid, is nowhere to be found." He sucked in a sharp breath. "and Calen is in ruins."

Darian's pale blue eyes grew paler. This was not good. There had been no warning of what might happen. No one had asked for help. Had there been no time? "What happened?"

Raul shook his head solemnly. "My friend, I was in the middle of it when it all happened. James told me about the insurgence that happened in Calen a century ago. He said the Werewolves were chained by the Vampires before the Druids arrived and set them free. However, between the two events, Adelaide the witch used the blood of the eldest Vampire, Marcus, to create a hybrid of both Vampire blood and wicked witchery. It—"

"Did you say Adelaide?" Darian interrupted.

"Yes, Adelaide."

Darian felt his hand ball into tight fists. "What happened in the insurgence? How did it end?"

"Adelaide escaped when the Druids captured and locked the hybrids behind a door they built in a place called the Dome. Now, after they've managed to keep it closed for more than a century, the door has been opened, and the hybrids are out in Calen." Raul continued talking about the story James had told him, but Darian's mind drifted elsewhere. His thoughts were fixated on Adelaide.

Finally, he thought. *I have found you at last, Adelaide.*

Chapter 4

Ryan lay with his face to one side, his black hair like the broken crown of a fallen king. His body was bruised and scarred. His clothes torn and barely covering his body. His pale face now possessed a slightly crooked nose, and his green irises were several shades darker, drowning in the pool of red that was fading through the whiteness 'round his eyes.

He lifted his head off the ground as Marcus approached, and though he was trying to stand up he failed to muster the strength to lift a bone from off the pebbles of the roof. It was as if he was drawn to the ground, as if he was being swallowed into the depths of the concrete that lay under the pebbles by some peculiar force of gravity that was alien to him. Ryan glanced down to his legs. At the knees, the lower half of his legs were just hanging, dangling like a piece of meat foreign to his body.

"Marcus," he uttered in something that sounded like a whisper, his voice barely audible, "Adelaide." He tried to speak, but his words weren't making their way through his rusty vocal chords.

"Stay still," Marcus said assertively as he knelt to examine Ryan's lower limbs.

There was a sudden crack and Ryan screamed out in a growl. It amplified through the forests and the lake behind them as Marcus corrected Ryan's dislocated legs.

"The full moon," Ryan said as his breath was caught in the pain of his torn body.

"When night falls," Marcus replied, standing and looking at the faraway towers of the city.

Ryan crawled toward the walls of the roof, dragging his legs behind him. He sat with his back to the wall and let out a sigh that came from the deepest parts of his soul. "Where's Atlanta?" he asked as the memories came crawling back to him.

"I thought you would have the answer to that question." Marcus said quietly, and after a moment continued, "The Skolars are missing. They haven't shown up since the beginning of all of this." The Vampire turned to look at him.

"Me?" Ryan asked in surprise. "Last I saw her, we were in the basement of her house, the night *you* apparently gave me a beating at the Dome."

"Of course you don't remember," Marcus replied, not in a scolding manner but more matter-of-fact. "It seems you've been compelled since then." He tilted his head slightly. "That was months ago, Ryan."

Months ago? Impossible. And yet, somehow his body seemed to make more sense of it than his head.

As night fell on the dreary roof of the building they sat on, the blazing full moon sat on the verge of taking its full form in the sky. Through their frustrated eyes, they watched the darkness take over the dust-swayed air of the city and swallow the pride of the daylight sky.

Little did Ryan know that with the full moon, not only was his strength returning to his weary limbs and muscles, but also the memories that would haunt him for years to come.

"What happened?" Marcus asked.

Ryan was about to answer when his voice caught in his throat.

At first, the memories appeared in his mind as flashes of a nightmare, blurry yet destined to be as animated as his own reflection in a mirror. The first memory was of his father's murder. That morning when his compulsion first took form. He remembered how he ran out of the house, hearing the howls of his father, and then finding his father's body lying in the grass, contaminated by the blue blood that encircled their backyard. Then came the hovering sounds of the hybrid that tore through Ryan's own limbs, its claws still carrying stains of his father's blood. There was the blur that followed; Skylar, or as the memories later whispered to him, Adelaide. He saw clearly how he was tossed into her wicked games like a stone thrown, just to sink into the depths of a darkened sea. His heart curled into itself in agony as he remembered kissing her in front of the one girl he knew he trusted. The one girl he would give anything to give his heart to.

Atlanta.

A whimper slipped through his lips. He wondered where she was. He gazed at the moon as it promised him more of the ugly story unfolding before his eyes. The flashes came like hurricanes storming into a broken city. He saw James' face as he was pressing him against the floor of the roof that he now sat on, blade in hand. He saw the hesitation in James' eyes, and he saw the last choice James made. The memory carried with it a scene that promised to haunt Ryan for years to come. James' eyes telling him that by not piercing the knife into his chest, he was giving him the responsibility to protect his niece.

It couldn't be. Ryan felt he was too weak. He'd never be able to protect Atlanta the way James had. He felt incapable of even saving himself from the claws of the dust in the wind.

He stared at the spot where Atlanta had fainted, her uncle's death resting within her tear-stained eyes. He wondered what might have happened had he been stronger, more in control, more like his father. *James would still be here.* He sighed deeply and tried to stand. His now-restored legs carried him effortlessly, healed under the bright gaze of the full moon.

There was no time to waste. He had to kill Adelaide and save a particular Druid from the witch's claws.

He looked at Marcus and his eyes burned. He began shifting, every bit of rage within him turning into tension in his own muscles. Every drop of blood shed because of him becoming a hair on his furry arms. His fangs elongated.

He stared Marcus in the eyes, and with a deep growl said, "I have to find Atlanta."

Marcus reached out and rested his hand on Ryan's broad shoulder. "*We* are going to find Atlanta."

Chapter 5

The misty green shores of Lisbon emitted an aura of mystery. The moon hung in the purple sky, serenaded by the whispering of the breeze. Some moments the wind would blow roughly in an attempt to entertain the company of the sand within its carriage, and in other moments it would call from the depths of the sea for a bathing of the starlight.

A stone arch bore down to the sea, its pillars immersed in the waters below. Darian sat on the edge of the arch in silence, looking out at the horizon. He saw the velvety purple sky and the sea merge as one, like two sets of fingers perfectly entwined. For him it didn't resemble a specific desire or a metaphor of anything profound. Rather, the calmness of the ends of those forces of nature helped his mind sink deeper into contemplation.

He and Raul had talked for hours in The Coven's headquarters. Raul shared the details of his story with Darian like a musical piece that escalated perfectly into climaxes of horror. The fall of Calen was not only a matter of a faraway city that fell to an alien form of supernatural hybrids, but a threat to every corner of the world. What was worse than the idea of a much more powerful form of Vampires and Witches was that they were all under the control of someone whose malicious mind was not foreign to Darian.

On the contrary; he knew it very well, and in the depths of his heart he both feared and longed to encounter it.

Darian sent Raul to America to retrace the steps of the settlements of Vampires and Werewolves. But Darian was looking for something different. He wanted to find a specific evil that he knew was lurking somewhere in the distant continent.

Years before that the same evil had been a visitor in his own city, and though insignificant damage had been done it had left with one success: it had taken away Darian's mother. To him, it was but a foggy memory that hid in the core of his subconscious mind. Sometimes the nightmares would bring him scenes of the day when he saw the dark green mist surrounding the witch, her back to him as his mother uttered her last scream.

He tried to drive the thought and memory away. Instead, he focused every tiny atom of boiling blood raging within him and imagined all that darkness merging with the entwined forces of the sea and the sky in the distance.

I've finally found you, Adelaide. And this time, there will be no hiding.

A raging tidal wave of desire rose within him, a need for vengeance like no other. However, Darian was wiser than to surrender his senses to the temptations of it. Instead, he knew he needed calmness. He needed his mind working well, both when he was attending it and also when he'd be elsewhere, away from the ramblings of his thoughts.

He lowered his gaze and the starry distance ahead of him was met with his bowing head, as if to tear away the scenes attacking him like feral waves to his spine. He looked at his palms as his fingers involuntarily closed into fists. He breathed deeply and allowed his hands to be the only part of him that showed his anger.

From behind him came the sound of stones crunching under feet, and he turned. In the darkness, Raul appeared at the arch, slowly walking his way.

Darian thought of how, right when he'd been trying to control the reflexes of his body to the tyranny of anger within him, his friend came strolling up with a grin on his face, as if holding the veil that would dim the brightness of his vivid nightmares. As Raul neared him, he thought of how serenity comes, carried by a friend, when your own mind tries to become an enemy of your own.

Darian dangled his feet from the edge of the arch as Raul settled next to him, and the two sat in silence, gazing out at the sea.

"Did you see her?" Darian asked, his eyes still fixed on the distant horizon.

"Atlanta?" replied Raul. "Saw her, but didn't talk to her. She's beautiful, though," he added, smiling and laughing silently at his own misplaced humor.

Darian grinned and picked up a small rock, then threw it into the sea ahead of him. The stone sank right in without bouncing off the surface. "I meant Adelaide."

Raul's smile turned into a slightly distressed look as he observed the rage that swirled in Darian's blue eyes. "No one did," he replied. "You know how Witches hide and lurk only in shadows. Just like those ugly Vampires in the east."

Darian smiled, knowing that Raul was trying to comfort him by attacking the Witches and Vampires. The two friends never talked about his mother's murder. However, it was a grief shared silently between them.

"There was something else I forgot to mention earlier," Raul said suddenly. "There were flying beasts in the skies of the city right before I left. They had grey wings, and set fire to what was underneath them by dropping a kind of black tar from their mouths. It was horrifying. James told me about them in his story of the insurgence. He said they were—"

"Gargoyles," Darian interrupted him. "My father told me about them years back. He said they were also another creation of the Witches, centuries ago. In the time of the voyages they were cemented and made into statues sold around the world as decorations."

"I can't imagine..." Raul shook his head, "what the people in Calen must be going through."

"I doubt there's room for imagination now. I think we must act as soon as possible," Darian replied, masking his rage in a tone of confidence.

Raul stared at Darian as he shifted from his previous hidden anger to a sudden composure and self-assurance accompanied with a grin. He could ask what Darian thought, if he considered sending others to help, or what The Coven should do. Instead, he asked, "When are you going?"

Darian again looked out into the distance, as if consulting the stars. He held a couple of stones in his hand, and shook them in his fist as if playing with dice. He threw the stones into the water, and this time they bounced several times on the surface before sinking into the depths of the sea.

He'd already figured Calen couldn't be left to its ruin. Not only because the danger in the city was a threat to every part of the world, not only because of the responsibilities that weighed down on him...not only because his father had entrusted him with the duties The Coven was expected to fulfill.

It was also because he couldn't shake the scene of his mother's murder from his mind. He knew no matter how much he looked down on vengeance and how much he despised the rage that was lurking in his veins, he still had to act in accordance with his heart, mind, and body. He knew he had to end the centuries'-long reign of Adelaide's malevolence, even though he had no idea how.

Darian stood, catching one last glimpse of the clasping of sky onto the sea. "In the morning, I'll be heading to America, to Calen."

"No," Raul said quietly, starting down at the long drop to the sea.

"No? What? You're going to try to stop me?"

Raul shook his head. "No, friend. Tomorrow, *we're* heading to Calen. Together."

Chapter 6

*G*et up!

Atlanta's eyes fluttered open, slowly and painfully, her vision a blur. She could feel her heart pounding in her chest, calm and steady, yet weak. Every inch of her body tingled, and her muscles felt like deadweights on top of her, pressing her down to the ground.

Get up!

She groaned and tried to move her head, but could only lift it a few inches off the ground. She turned it slowly, shifting her position only enough to convince herself that she still could, and gazed at the silhouettes of the candles a few feet away from her.

For a few seconds, she tried to remember where she was.

"Rise and shine, princess."

The room was too dark for her to see who was talking, but the voice was instantly recognizable. She felt a shudder race through her, her mind screaming silent warnings she couldn't comprehend.

"Planning on staying there forever? Giving up?" James Skolar stepped out of the shadows and crouched down in front of her.

She could see him smile in the darkness, and she instinctively smiled back. "Where are we?" she muttered, coughing violently as the air she breathed in scratched her throat. *Why is my mouth so dry?*

"You're in the Dome," James replied. "Don't you remember?"

Atlanta frowned, scouring her mind for the remains of any memory that would shed light onto why she was here. She couldn't remember coming to the Dome, let alone falling asleep on the cold floor beneath her. Placing both hands by her side, she slowly pushed herself up onto her knees.

"There you go." James chuckled. "That's my girl."

"How long have I been out?" Atlanta shivered, but not from the cold.

"I'm not really sure," James replied. "It's hard to tell down here."

Atlanta looked up at her uncle. "Down here?"

James shrugged. "Well, we're not exactly in the Dome proper, sweetie. We're about two stories below it."

Atlanta shifted so she was sitting with her back to the wall, her head swimming as her body threatened to topple over. A raging headache began at the back of her skull, and she could feel its tendrils snaking their way to the front. "There's nothing below the Dome." Was she speaking the words clearly? They seemed slurred to her somehow.

"You know better than that." James *tsk*ed. "But I'll give you a few seconds. It'll all come back to you."

Atlanta's frown deepened, and just as the headache engulfed her a kaleidoscope of images flashed before her eyes.

She saw the towers first, the green mist above her head, and Skylar smiling at her from a distance. Only, it wasn't Skylar. She knew that, but for some strange reason she couldn't put a name to the face. The images darkened, and for a split second she believed she had been spared the agony of watching any more.

And just as she took a deep breath of relief, the images shot through her head again. She saw James and Ryan fighting. Her uncle's hesitation. The hybrids' attack.

Atlanta closed her eyes and shook her head violently. "N-No!" she stammered.

"Atlanta."

She kept her eyes glued shut, willing the voice away, unable to make peace with what she knew was true.

"Look at me, baby," James whispered.

Atlanta felt the tears sting her eyes and roll down her cheeks. Reluctantly, she opened them and looked at her uncle. He smiled at her, and it only broke her heart even more.

"I'm right here," he said reassuringly.

Atlanta sobbed. "No, you're not," she whispered. "You're dead."

James's smile widened. "Well, that can be argued." He chuckled. "Physically, sure, but here..." he pointed to his heart and then to hers, "I'm very much alive right there."

"Is that supposed to make me feel better?"

James shrugged. "It should be a little reassuring. Nobody ever truly dies, Atlanta. You keep them alive as long as you need them."

Atlanta's vision blurred as more tears obscured it. "I need you now."

"Which is pretty much why I'm here."

Atlanta took a deep breath and let it out in a whimper. "Uncle James."

"Right now, there are more important things to do," James interjected, cutting through her thoughts. "Like getting out of here, for starters. Do you think you can walk?"

Atlanta ran a hand across her crimson suit, now caked in mud and torn in various places. She wiggled her toes, flexed her ankles, and moved her legs. She felt them tingle, and firmly pushed herself to her feet. "I can walk."

"That's my girl," James said. "Now, let's find our way back to the surface, okay?"

Atlanta hesitated, looking at the circle of candles that were surrounding her uncle's corpse. Her body shuddered at the memory, and she quickly pushed her shoulders back. Now was not the time. She stared at the opening of the corridor, the darkness there even more menacing than that which surrounded her. "That way," she said, pointing.

"That way, indeed," James replied.

Atlanta moved forward. Her legs were unsteady and her mind played tricks on her, but she was determined to keep walking. It didn't matter whether James was a figment of her imagination; her uncle had a sound argument. She had to find her way back and warn the others.

Warn them about what?

"The door," Atlanta whispered.

"Try not to think of that right now," James said from behind her.

Even though she knew he was right, it was all she could think about.

She remembered the voices behind the door, how her body had seemed to operate on its own. She remembered the spell she'd been under—she'd been compelled to do what she'd spent her life fighting not to do. DON'T OPEN THE DOOR.

She wasn't herself when it happened, she knew that, but it didn't make the guilt eating at her any less agonizing. She should've been strong enough to resist. Strong enough to stop it. Uncle James should've been helping her. Instead, he'd let himself be killed.

Something crunched under her boot and she jumped back, instinctively reaching for her sword. In the darkness she could see the outline of the dead raven she'd stepped on; further down the corridor, more of the same. Her eyes had adjusted to the darkness, and the long corridor appeared to be littered with hundreds of dead birds.

"Keep going," James said from behind her, and she felt a force on her back pushing her forward.

She made her way down the corridor, careful not to step on any more ravens. When she turned the corner, her eyes fell on the open door and the darkness that loomed behind it.

She stopped, her gaze fixated on the dead space that had once confined the hybrids. They were gone now. She knew that with every fiber of her being. They were all out, terrorizing the city above—destroying the place she called home.

"Are you okay?" James asked.

Atlanta nodded and turned to look at a staircase leading up. "I'm fine," she snapped. "Any idea what's waiting on the other side of that wall?"

"Only one way to find out."

Atlanta made her way up the stone stairs, and as she reached the wall that separated the underground tunnel from the Dome proper she pulled out her sword. Her hand found the bricks easily, almost as if working from instinct, and the wall slid open.

A gush of wind welcomed her, sand and light mixing and bombarding her, blinding her completely and forcing her to stagger back. It was as if she had stepped into a storm. It took a while for the winds to die down as they filled the underground tunnels that had previously been spared their wrath.

"I'm right here," James assured her, and Atlanta used that little bit of confidence to push her way out into the Dome.

Nothing could have prepared her for what she saw.

The ground was littered with the corpses of fallen Vampires and Werewolves, some greatly mangled, others staring with dead eyes into space. The Dome itself looked like The Cast of Mother Nature had come down on it. The glass ceiling was gone, the walls on several sides crumbled, tables and chairs shattered and strewn everywhere. Whatever had happened here, it had been devastating, and the weight of it all fell heavily on Atlanta.

This is all because of me.

"Careful, Druid," James hissed from behind her.

Atlanta fell to one knee instantly, holding her sword up as her eyes darted left and right.

Several pairs of glowing red eyes stared back at her. A manic cackle sounded to her left, and the hiss of anger filled what remained of the

Dome. The eyes came closer, and through the veil of sand and wind bodies materialized before her.

"Vampires?" Atlanta whispered.

"Humans," James replied. "It doesn't matter. They're compelled and just as dangerous."

Atlanta stood slowly. She heard the soft rustle of running feet, and turned just in time as a figure pounced out of the storm at her. She swung her sword expertly, swiftly, her muscles screaming at the strain.

The body crumpled by her feet.

"It begins," James said. "Careful, Atlanta. Remember what I taught you."

Seeing she'd survived the first attack, others lunged at her.

Atlanta held her ground, waiting for them to come closer before pushing herself forward and slicing through the next two attackers. Screams echoed through the Dome, and from behind her she could hear more footsteps racing towards her.

She swirled, letting one hand drop from her sword just in time to release a pair of knives and throw them into the mist. Screams of pain let her know she'd found her targets, and she quickly made her way through another pair of attackers, their blood splattering her crimson suit.

And still they came.

She jumped out of the way of hands trying to grab her and sprinted into the main hall. The winds were weaker here, the dust less dense, and in the clearing she could see she was now surrounded by at least two dozen compelled humans, all racing towards her with incredible speed.

"They're too many," she gasped.

"You've got this," James replied.

But she knew that wasn't true. She was tired, her muscles aching and her mind foggy. She could probably withstand another minute or two of attacks, but that would only serve to slow down her predators, not subdue them all.

She had to come up with a better plan.

A hand grabbed her shoulder, and she slammed her elbow back and into the man's face, turning and slicing through his chest as he fell. Her eyes searched for an escape, any way to rid herself of the confinements of the Dome. She could deal with all this better if she had more room, if she could separate the masses.

To her right, the crumbled remains of a wall offered just that escape.

Atlanta was about to turn, when a blinding burst of green light shot through the entirety of the Dome. She fell to one knee and covered her face, feeling the heat of the green light envelop her and race past her. Screams sounded in the air, and from somewhere to her left a body exploded in a shower of blood.

And then, just as suddenly as it had started, the light disappeared.

Atlanta lowered her arm from her face, her hand tightening on the pommel of her sword, ready to face this new challenge. Her breathing grew labored as her eyes adjusted to the dim light, taking in the carnage of burned bodies around her.

Across the main hall, two figures made their way to her.

"Uncle?" she whispered. "Do I fight? Or run?"

But James was silent.

Slowly, she pushed herself to her feet, raising her sword high, ready to strike. They weren't human, she could sense that right away. But there was something... different about them. She set her legs shoulder-width apart, ready to fight—or die trying. "I'm not letting you win," she called out, trying to scare them. "I'm stronger than you think."

The two figures, both male, did not stop.

She locked her elbow into place, trying to decide which one to strike first. Which would be weaker? She hesitated when she saw one of the men smile at her.

"Atlanta Skolar," the man said, his foreign accent thick against the wind in the Dome.

Her eyes dropped down to his hands.

They were still glowing green from the magic he'd just unleashed. "It's a pleasure to finally meet you." He stopped in front of her and clasped his hands behind his back. "Allow me to introduce myself. I'm Darian. Leader of The Coven."

Chapter 7

Atlanta stared at the intoxicating man in front of her.

It was like being in the corner of a fully acoustic room where the echo of your whisper dances, leaps, and falls off the ceiling, into your ears. Like the sound of several machines the second when the power is cut off and the last few electrons run their way through the closed circuit to escape the abyss of the power shortage. Similar to the line between consciousness and the lack of it in the seconds between the rambling thoughts of a head lying on a bed in a dark room during the final ticks of midnight, and that one thought which lingers in the sleeping mind. Or more like gazing at eyes captured in the deep blue of the sky right before the heavy clouds of autumn come strolling by and obscure the loudness of the wavelengths of light blue.

That was how Atlanta felt when her eyes settled on Darian. She didn't speak it, but he could feel her every thought race through her head.

"I've heard a lot about you." Darian cocked his head to one side, as if uncertain she was listening to him. "My friend Raul knows your uncle."

Knew my uncle. He's dead. She suddenly felt lost, her knees shaking as her mind tingled with some foreign feeling inside of her, a feeling she probably never even realized she felt, or had forgotten in the midst of the loss of reality that followed. Somehow, she'd lost her voice. Maybe it was realizing her uncle was gone. Or that she wasn't alone. She felt this stranger called Darian probed her mind, trying to find the words she couldn't seem to utter, and a wall instantly shot up against him.

Darian frowned and tried again, apparently unaccustomed to being shut out in this manner. But with all his intelligence and his skill, piercing her eyes with his mind's persistent needles, he couldn't break through.

He looked at Raul, who only shrugged. His friend mouthed the word *shock*, and then returned his gaze to Atlanta.

Her heart pounded quickly, and her chest heaved as she tried to catch her breath. She sensed Darian could feel the strain she was going through, the confusion mixed with uncertainty that engulfed her. Then, the pounding ceased. Her eyelids suddenly grew heavy, though she tried to keep them open. She was going to faint. Her body dropped like a feather as her arms flailed around.

Her elbows rested on Darian's arms as he rushed to intercept her. "Raul!"

The other man rushed to his side, helping him as they tried to keep Atlanta steady. She fought against the darkness but couldn't seem to overcome it.

She felt Darian lift her, catching a quick glimpse of her eyes as they fluttered open and then half closed again. He turned and looked at Raul, but his friend didn't seem at all surprised at the state she was in.

She knew she was frail and her skin pale. Her crimson suit was dusty and covered in blood. It was shadowed by the gray that brushed itself over the back of his suit.

"She seems to have been here a while," Raul said as he stood behind Darian, taking in the utter devastation of the Dome.

Atlanta heard their conversation, as if in a dream. She had nothing left in her, except to fight to stay semi-conscious.

"She needs food, and water." Darian added in a whisper, "We have to take her somewhere safe."

"There's one place that should still be safe for the time being," Raul declared, his voice sounding weary, as if afraid of more attackers. "The basement of her house."

"Let's go." Darian swung around, and Atlanta felt the room continue to spin long after he'd stopped.

"James told me there's a secret passage in their basement, leading to tunnels under the city, but we have to figure out how to find it."

Darian only nodded, and Raul began to lead him out of the Dome.

Atlanta felt only a little heat on her face, thinking that the sun may have already set. She didn't know that it was still obscured by the dust that reigned over the city. She fought against the waves of darkness begging to take her away, and forced her eyes to open. It took everything last bit of strength she had to gaze at the horizon. Something bitterly peculiar was taking over. Green mist lit the swollen clouds, and everything that was above them turned several shades darker. It was as if seeds had been scattered across the bed of the sky and were shooting their roots upwards in fingers of lightning. Atlanta let her eyes fall shut as Darian carried her, marching behind the other man leading the way. There was no comfort in what she saw, and it was clear that, come night, the city would be forced to endure a wave of deadly attacks.

She tried to figure out what the sky was trying to warn her of. Maybe it was a dream. But she knew better. She knew who was now in control of the city, what wicked force was at play. *Adelaide.*

She felt the man's hands clench into fists, heating up with rage. She sensed his thoughts as she finally gave into the darkness.

I'm going stop you, Adelaide, he promised. *I will bring an end to your reign of terror.*

Chapter 8

For days, Atlanta lay surrounded by nothing but the silence of the dark underground, and the bleeding of her mind. She felt a void take the place of her heart, and when she tried to fill it with memories or a glimmer of hope her mind would fail her, and she'd end up with a heart filled with the trembles of bitter emotions.

She was lost, forgotten, failing to even recognize her own self.

The bitterness in Atlanta's heart was the product of a series of happenings which had her question why she'd ever replaced resentment with patience and content. She was a fool, and would spend the rest of her days resenting herself for letting the person who caused James' death into her life.

She used me. She played me. She knew exactly what to do and when.

She realized everything that lay outside the Dome and in the ruins of the city was for her eyes to see, for her mind to contemplate, and for her conscience to bear. She was being punished. Even though she knew she had been under some spell when she'd opened the door, she still heard the voices in her ears and had opened the door with her own hand.

This is all my fault. I don't deserve to wake up.

Except I'm hiding now. This is my fault. I can't hide from that.

Her mind flooded with obscure thoughts, and suddenly she felt like she could sense the touch of warm air on her skin. The fog in her mind began dissipating, and she slowly felt herself rise out of the abyss she had been settling in.

Where am I?

She didn't dare open her eyes, fearing that she might wake up to find herself still in that wretched place beneath the Dome, lying on the cold ground, inches away from the circle of candles. This time James wouldn't be with her, though. She would be alone.

But a part of her was sure that wasn't the case. She felt a sudden sense of familiarity and an odd feeling of security that she hadn't felt in some time. She could sense the smell of books mixed with the aroma of the leather that soaked the basement of her house. She opened her eyes slowly, the lights blinding her for a moment and the fluorescence beamed through every corner and in every direction.

A shadow was forming on the ceiling above her, almost as if the light was coming out of her own body and reflecting off an object right above her. As the blur began sharpening, she recognized it was a face.

For a second, her heart nearly jumped out of her chest. As if it was all another one of those malicious tricks that her mind entertained. James' face was unmistakable, gazing down at her with concern in his eyes. His face shone from the sides, and his deep-brown eyes glittered. Slowly, his features darkened, and his eyes turned to a deep blue.

"Raul, she's waking up."

A second shadow came into view, but Atlanta barely noticed it. She was captivated by the deep blue gazing down at her. Her vision sharpened, and she looked at the face of the man from the Dome, the man who had introduced himself as Darian.

"Easy," Darian whispered. "Don't make any sudden moves. What's left of your strength is barely keeping you alive."

She realized she lay on the couch beside the bookshelves in the basement of her house. Both men were standing above her, their eyes fixed on her own. It took her a minute before she recognized the slim figure of Raul, and her mind related him to that morning he was with

James in the living room of their house. Even though Darian's face was still alien to her, there was something about his leaning over her that brought comfort to both her sleeping and her now-awakened mind.

Her eyes opened wide and she felt as if a weight had been lifted off her chest. She alternated glances at the two men standing above her, then turned her eyes towards the books, then the training area. The weight that had been lifted off her chest suddenly returned, the memories rushing back to her like feral waves down her spine. She turned towards Darian again.

He had his back to her and was saying something to Raul, but her ears had still not started functioning properly and the voices were nothing more than muffled whispers.

Darian turned again and stared at her, his lips moving. She cocked her head to one side, confused. She couldn't make out what he was saying.

His words became soft whispers, and the whispers seemed as if they were being spoken under water. She felt them crawling up her spine and brushing the back of her neck like goose bumps. The voice was processed by her sense of touch and not her hearing, and once it reached her ears the frequency of the sound peaked and reached a horrendous crescendo. The pain resonated through her brain like the stabbing of a thousand knives. She screamed, and jumped from where she was lying and onto the floor. She leaned her back against the bottom of the couch and held her ears with both hands.

Darian and Raul came rushing forward and leaned down in surprise.

"Are you okay?" Darian asked calmly as he bent down and rested his right hand on her shivering shoulders.

Atlanta froze as her body suddenly let go of all pain. *Did he just do that?* She shook her head slowly. It was probably only a coincidence. "I-I'm fine," Atlanta replied thickly. "I'm okay. I think."

She tried to brush away the concern that her mind confused with pity, but her body did not even attempt to shake off his hands from her shoulders.

Raul stood and took a few steps back, and she was thankful of the small gesture that made her feel less cornered. He gazed at Darian who, in turn, signaled with his head towards the table on the other side. Raul disappeared into the periphery of her vision, then returned with a glass of water.

Darian took the glass from him and offered it to Atlanta, who hesitated before reaching for it with shaking hands. She looked from Darian to Raul, and suddenly felt helpless. She shook Darian's hand off her shoulder, her strength returning in waves.

Now is the time. She stood, drank the water quickly, then made her way towards the training area. She needed weapons and to test her strength before going out to find Adelaide.

Darian hurried after her. "I'm sure this is very confusing, us being in your home and all. But I assure you, we mean you no harm."

"You were at the Dome." Atlanta shrugged. It felt like a dream from long ago.

"Yes, we were," Darian replied. "We brought you here after you fainted. Allow me to introduce myself once more."

She stared into the emptiness of the walls, and still with her back turned to him, she sighed softly. "Darian," she whispered.

"You remember?"

Atlanta merely nodded.

"Then you know Raul?"

"My uncle introduced him to me, briefly."

"I'm sorry about your uncle." Darian's voice dropped. "I understand you and he were close."

Atlanta suddenly felt like she couldn't hold onto her composure any longer, and her knees began to shake. The mention of her uncle's name by another person made his absence even more real. Her eyes stung with tears, and she felt one roll down her cheek.

Yet she maintained the stiffness of her voice and breathed in the dust-free air. She wanted to turn around and face the man who had so easily made himself at home in her house, but she couldn't. Not like this. Not with tears in her eyes. "Who are you?"

"I'm Darian."

She waved her hand. "I know that. *Who* are you?"

Darian cleared his throat. "The Coven."

Atlanta nearly laughed. "The Coven's a myth. It doesn't exist."

It was Darian's turn to scoff. "We exist when we're needed," he replied. "When the real world and that which we try to keep hidden collide. As it has in Calen."

Atlanta felt something scratch the inside of her head. Darian's words left more questions than answers. Flashes of her battle in the Dome played across her eyes, and in the midst of them all a bright green burst of fire.

"The hybrids," she whispered.

"I know," Darian said. "I've been briefed on what happened."

There was no use hiding what had happened. Whatever Darian knew, he didn't know it all. "I let them out," she suddenly declared. "I opened the door."

"Atlanta," Darian whispered as he reached for her hand. "I can feel you've been drowning in a spell your conscience is casting on you, but you must stop binding yourself by it."

What the hell? "Binding myself?" she sputtered as she spun around, jerking her wrist free and letting her hands ball into angry fists. "It's called being honest with oneself. I saw the Dome. I saw the world outside. You think I'm going to hide the fact that this is all my fault?"

"The dust is Adelaide's," Darian said. "The ruins are her making. You were used to open the door. You didn't open it. You didn't plan it. Your conscience is a labyrinth you're trapping yourself in, and your mind will not stop before dragging your heart behind it like a dim shadow."

Where the heck was this guy from? Atlanta's eyes widened and she glanced towards Raul. "Does he always talk like this?"

"Atlanta," Darian said, regaining her attention. "I can feel that you blame yourself for what's happening in Calen. But you shouldn't."

"You don't know what happened," Atlanta hissed. "Why are you talking as if you were there, as if you were inside my head?"

"You're right." Darian nodded. "I have no clue what's lurking inside your mind, but looking at you now, hearing your voice, seeing the tears in your eyes, I know what's in your heart."

Atlanta stared in silence as his words found their way through her mind and to her heart. For a moment, she blocked what she was hearing because she knew it was softening the bitterness that had taken over her. She didn't need comfort. She needed anger. She needed the fuel that would push her. And Darian wasn't helping. "You know nothing about me," she said. "Leave me alone." She turned away from him and walked towards the stairs leading up to the house. She could see Raul head to intercept her and she stopped, eyeing him carefully, her gaze as threatening as her stance.

"Let her go," Darian said.

Atlanta's eyes narrowed as she looked from one man to the other. "And get the hell out of my house."

Without waiting for a reply, she made her way upstairs.

Chapter 9

*"D*_{*on't."*}

Atlanta didn't hear Uncle James. Well, she heard him but just chose to ignore him. She didn't even try to acknowledge his ghost-like whispering. She scanned the destruction around her, falling on one pile of debris after the other. The sand slapped against her face, her hair blowing around her head as she took in the scene before her.

Her home was gone. The place she'd grown up in, fell asleep to the sounds of the maple outside scraping against her window, convinced her uncle not to cook and just order in. All that remained was a skeleton of a place that once used to be her haven; all that remained were ghosts of memories.

"Don't."

Atlanta turned to look at her uncle. James stood where the living room had once been. Three walls still stood, the third crumbled in a pile where parts of the second floor had collapsed. Only the couch remained, mangled under layers of dust. The rest of the furniture was gone.

"Don't what?" she whispered, almost to herself.

James dusted a part of the couch and sat down, crossing one leg over the other. He watched her as she took in what remained of her home. Dried blood was strewn across the walls of the hallway leading to the kitchen, and from where she stood she almost laughed at the sight of the stove standing tall with no wall behind it.

"I know what you're thinking," James said. "And I'm telling you, don't."

Atlanta felt tears well up in her eyes. Her hands rolled into tight fists, and she could feel her body shake in a mix of anger, frustration, and loss. "This shouldn't have happened."

"But it did," James replied. "That's why I'm telling you, don't blame yourself. What's done is done. Right now, we have to think about what to do next. What to do to fix the situation."

Atlanta's eyes burned, her tears leaving dark streaks as they rolled down the dust on her cheeks. She could feel the wind picking up, the storm around her intensifying, as if growing with her growing anger. "I'm going to kill her," she hissed. "I'm going to find her and rip her apart. First I'll tear her heart out."

James coughed, and scratched his beard. "I believe you, but let me remind you that there was very little you could do against Adelaide before. You need more than just your training."

Atlanta looked at her uncle and frowned. "She caught me off guard," she said tersely. "I won't make that mistake again."

"Yes, you will," James smiled at her, a loving smile, a fatherly smile that made her heart ache for the real him to be there, not just a wraith her mind was conjuring. "You went in high on emotions, and that's exactly what you're doing now. This'll only end the same way it did before. Except, this time, Adelaide won't be as generous with your life."

"I'll be better prepared this time," Atlanta insisted.

"No, you won't," James replied. "You haven't even noticed the Werewolf behind you."

Atlanta smiled at her uncle, her eyes darkening, a heat burning in them she had never felt before. "Actually, I did."

In one quick movement Atlanta drew her sword, fell to one knee and spun around, swinging upwards. Her blade swished through the storm around her, the thick sand obscuring her vision, her senses taking over. A terrible growl sounded above her head, and a heavy thud followed. In the swirl of sand, a paw fell into view.

Her eyes burned hotter, and before she stood up she pulled one of her knives out of her belt and threw it towards the kitchen. She watched it fly towards nothing, spinning quickly in the air. Then, just as it flew over the threshold, a second Wolf appeared. The knife struck home and sent the beast to the ground.

Atlanta stood up and walked towards the fallen Wolf. Her uncle appeared in the kitchen, gazing down in confusion at the fallen beast.

"They were waiting for you," he said.

Atlanta bent down and pulled the knife out. "There are more coming."

"You're sure?"

She nodded, sheathing her weapons and turning to make her way back to the basement. From the corner of her eye she saw a shadow move, red eyes burning in the storm, then quickly disappearing. From the speed of the visitor, she knew it was a Vampire.

Since when do they willingly work together?

"They're compelled," James said as she opened the door. He was standing on the other side, leaning against the banister, scratching his beard and staring at the ceiling in contemplation.

Atlanta didn't reply. She turned and locked the door from the inside. It would give them some time if any others decided to come into the house—or what was left of the house. She spun around and made her way down the stairs, Darian and Raul followed her. Once in the basement she opened a weapon cupboard and picked the ones she needed. Darian and Raul stood almost frozen as they watched her. She could sense their uneasiness.

She ignored them and moved past where they stood, opening the secret passage to the underpart of the basement. *So help if anyone or anything's down here.* She doubted it, but the thought crossed her mind anyway. She stepped into the vestibule and fell to where the bikes were supposed to be parked. On her left was the table where James normally sat, either working on the bikes' mechanics or creating sharper weapons.

She felt a surge of feelings creep up on her as she saw the shadow of James standing over the table, the sweat accumulating on the side of his forehead and his arms wrapped around the end of an arrow. She couldn't tell if she was remembering him, or if he was actually standing there, her mind playing tricks on her as it had been doing ever since she had stepped out of the tunnels in the Dome.

"You've gotta stop popping up like that," she mumbled.

"Apparently you still need me," James replied.

She walked over to his workstation, examining the weapons he'd been last working on. There was a series of blades that were curved in various ways. One of the blades had its edges curved like a concave lens, its tip unsharpened, with a slit on the tip where another thick sheet of metal could've been fitted in. There was something about all the weapons that was peculiar, but formed a pattern that she was beginning to understand.

All the arrows and blades were lined with a green metal that glowed like an emerald but felt more like a steely knife. There were three guns that looked more like nail guns than usual pistols. They were surrounded by bullets that were cylindrical and thin on both ends. The bullets were like the edges of the rest of the weapons, made of the same green material.

She knew the green resembled some sort of magic. She remembered James had started working on these weapons at the same time she had first told him about the red, glaring eyes of the compelled attackers on the football field of Calen High. The connection was instantly made in her head. James must've been working on weapons that could possibly be of some effect against the hybrids. She glared at the table. She clearly wasn't equipped with the knowledge of what they did.

What am I going to do with these?

"You have friends outside," James replied. "I'm sure they could figure it out."

"I don't trust them."

"You don't have to." James smiled. "Right now, it's enough to help you survive."

She felt her eyes burn again.

"Speaking of which," James glanced behind them, "I think it's time you actually got out of here."

Chapter 10

Darian and Raul sat in silence. They weren't leaving. At least they weren't going anywhere without Atlanta. No matter what she wanted or said to them. They sat at opposite ends of the couch, each lost in their thoughts. Once in a while Darian would stand and walk around, softly and slowly, his eyes taking in every light in the basement and his mind alternating between thoughts about what should be done next and the conversation he'd had with Atlanta. Even though their conversation was brief, it made him wonder about her. Something was different about this Druid. He just didn't know what.

"I think we have to leave the city now," Raul declared suddenly. "With how it is outside, there's no way we can find Adelaide let alone kill the countless hybrids on our own."

"I agree we're outnumbered and out-powered, but leaving now means we risk returning to the ashes of this city later," Darian replied. He wanted the witch destroyed, or captured at the very least, but how were they going to do it?

"But staying only means that we foolishly overestimate our ability. We can't possibly fight on our own. Even if Atlanta is capable of fighting the hybrids with us, we're still out-powered. And we don't know what Adelaide has planned. We're too...vulnerable."

Darian returned to the couch and sat heavily, leaning on his knees and looking at the floor. He lifted his head and looked at Raul. "If we

53

leave, we can call for more Druids to come, but by the time they arrive I fear it'll be too late to save the city. I fear the hybrids will go beyond Calen," he said. "We must make sure they're contained in Calen."

"And how can we possibly do that?" Raul stood.

"We have to stop them here. And get help."

"Are you saying one of us should stay in the city while the other leaves?"

"No!" Darian shook his head. "That cannot happen. We have to be together, the two of us. United, we can stand against her. And now it has become the three of us." Darian pointed at the wall where the secret passage to the basement was. "I believe she needs us as much as we need her."

"So, what do we do?"

Darian lifted his eyes to the ceiling bathed with the fluorescent lights. "We can't risk losing Adelaide's trail. The witch has a habit of disappearing whenever someone's on to her."

"If we stay here, she'll realize exactly where we are. We're sitting ducks." Raul sighed and ran his hand through his hair.

"And we've nowhere to hide or protect ourselves. Hiding in a basement or sneaking around in Calen isn't going to do us any favors." Darian pressed his lips tight together a moment. "You were right. We should leave the city, call on the forces from the north. We could be back in here in less than a week. Hopefully Adelaide won't realize we're gone. That might give us some time."

"Why not call on the Druids back home?" Raul asked.

"I've sent them all to Armenia, remember?"

"But the Druids in the north have been dormant for a long time. All the Vampires and Werewolves have settled here in this city. Up north there are barely any forces to help us." Raul didn't try to hide the frustration in his voice.

They were deep in conversation, each arguing that it was better to leave, and then arguing why they should stay and fight. Not sure who to call up for help. So engrossed in their argument were they, that they didn't notice Atlanta come back into the room. Darian glanced over and blinked in surprise.

She stood with her shoulder pressed against the wall that opened to the passage to the basement. Her hair resting on her left shoulder and her arms were folded. "Everlore," her voice came, piercing to their ears as she started walking towards them.

"Everlore? Isn't that a city far west?" asked Raul in confusion.

"No, that's another city. The Everlore I'm talking about is a town about sixty miles north of Calen. Uncle James told me the town had as many settlements of Vampires and Werewolves as Calen did. If Adelaide hasn't been there first, then we have a good chance of finding people to fight alongside us."

"And how can we be sure there's anyone still there?" Raul glanced at Darian, who could only shrug in response. He didn't know.

Atlanta shrugged. "I can't. But right now, what other option do we have?"

Darian sighed, looking back and forth between Raul and Atlanta, both watching him—waiting for him to make the final decision. "It's worth a shot," he finally said. "What do you know about the town?"

"Nothing more than the few things my uncle told me," Atlanta said. "There's definitely something mystical about it. How it's stayed under the radar for so long, no one can really tell. Marcus was fond of referring to it whenever he felt Calen was getting too crowded."

Darian frowned. *Why do I not know more about this place?*

"His words, not mine," Atlanta said.

"Well, we can't stay here," Raul cut in. "The longer we do, the more liable we are to be discovered."

Darian pondered the plan, closing his eyes as he tried to work out every possible angle and plan for the worst-case scenario. He suddenly nodded and looked at Atlanta. "How do we get there?"

Atlanta gestured to the secret passage. "The tunnels extend to the outskirts of Calen. From there we can take the highway leading to the forests around Everlore."

"If nothing gets in our way," Raul muttered.

Darian shot him a warning look. Except he saw Raul's eyes were darting from corner to corner, his muscles tense, as if ready to react to some unknown danger. Darian had learned early on to trust his friend's instincts. "Then we go," Darian said. "Let's restock and move out."

"There's no time," Atlanta said.

He turned towards her and felt his own muscles tense. A glow burned in her eyes, one he'd never seen before. Instinctively he called upon his magic, feeling the flames course through his veins, ready to explode when he willed. Her eyes were burning, almost red. Was she possessed as well? He shifted, setting his feet shoulder-width apart, ready for anything.

"What is it?" Raul whispered frantically.

Darian turned to him, but before he could reply Atlanta said, "We have company."

The door to the basement burst off its hinges, flying down the staircase and crashing onto the basement floor. A gust of wind burst through the opening, carrying with it a tidal wave of dust. And through the dust, they came.

There were half a dozen of them, eyes blazing red, storming down the stairs and jumping over the bannister. Vampires and Werewolves alike came for them, teeth bared, hissing.

How did Raul miss their arrival? Darian was about to let his magic fly when Atlanta suddenly jumped into action, blocking his attack. He stepped back in anger, wheeling to find a new angle. From the corner of his eyes, he could see Raul trying to do the same. But Atlanta was quick, a blur of red between the monsters attacking, her eyes burning almost as red as theirs. Maybe even darker.

She cut through them with ease, throwing her knives while expertly weaving her sword. They fell around her, growling and screaming, thrashing and squirming. They came for her from all angles, and instead of finding flesh they found her steel. Darian watched with wide eyes as the last of the attackers fell at her feet.

Atlanta stood panting in the center of the basement, surrounded by the corpses of their attackers, her blade dripping with the blood of the dead.

Darian briefly turned to Raul, and saw the same look of astonishment on his face.

Atlanta turned, her eyes downcast, the red glow gone. She pulled her knives out of the dead bodies and sheathed her sword, then made her way to the secret passage. Her shoulder brushed against Darian's as she walked past him. "Try to keep up," she said, and disappeared into the darkness of the tunnels beyond.

Chapter 11

Everlore

Under the veil of blue sky there were as many shadows as there was light, as much blur as there was the sharp white of a proud moon. And underneath the misty haze that descended from the skies to the pavement, a window to where she stood watching over the town sat slightly open. The scent of the dew adorned with the fragrance of the willow trees seeped in from the open window and rushed to feed her senses as she inhaled deeply.

"You are beautiful," Lenore whispered to the night sky. "Lovely in all your finery." She stared at the moon and the shadows, and sighed heavily. "It's a shame the beauty never lasts."

She averted her eyes, briefly looking at her slender fingers and the rings that adorned them. She ran her hands across the long robe around her shoulders, the fabric swallowing the light of the moon and reflecting it in silver waves across her body. She turned her head to the side, staring at her complexion in the large mirror beside her, her tall frame encased in the reflective frame as if she were staring at a painting of herself. She allowed herself a small smile, then looked away.

The walls of the room were reddish-brown, alternating in shades according to how dusty the part of the wall was. And the dustiness of the wall was in accordance with how close it was to a window. It almost seemed like a painting perfected by nature's way of breathing in an isolated place. Except that it wasn't isolated; the town hadn't been empty of breath for centuries, yet the people in it would never step a foot in any direction other than that in which the earth and wind were going.

There were cracks in the walls that extended to the yellowish ceilings of the room. The moonlight would bathe those crevices at night, and the sun would help them in their path towards decay when morning came. There was a dark green desk on the side of the room, perpendicular to the window she was standing at. The desk had several papers on it that looked as if they had aged for as long as the willow trees outside had. The ink on them was fresh, though, glistening as it dried.

Lenore was oblivious to the dust and aging of the room as she walked away from the window, the wooden floor creaking with the movement of her feet. She sighed softly as she picked up a small wooden box from the desk. It was black, and when she opened it she stared at the ruby that sat on a small white cushion inside. The stone shimmered across her light grey eyes. She closed her eyes when the stone revealed its light to her, as if she were bathing in its warm glow.

With the light came memories, images flashing behind her closed lids. A young boy by the beach, smiling and running just inches from the lapping of the waves. A baby girl in a cot, waving her arms, smiling in a way that made the sunlight seem dim in contrast. Flames reaching out with deadly fingers, igniting the world around her. The images came one by one, then coalesced to form a mural in her mind. She felt an involuntary tremor race through her.

She gently closed the box and put it back in its place, then walked towards the other side of the room. Her cloak was draped behind her and skimmed the dusty wooden floor with each step she took. There were three hard-cover books hanging on the wall, parallel to each other at eye-level. When she reached them, the wind gusted in from a window to her right and pushed the bottom part of her cloak, twirling it around her leg. She gracefully let the cloak be. She moved her head with quiet calmness to gaze out the window at the skies far away. She smiled. It was as if she were assuring the wind that she knew what it was trying to tell her.

She blew the dust off the books one by one, with soft blows of air that flowed softly out of her small, cold lips. She started with the red book on the far left, then softly moved towards the black one in the middle, and then the grey book on the far right. On each book contained a symbol of a moon during one of its stages on the cover. A crescent moon on the book to the left, a full moon on the black one, and a half moon on the book to the right.

She freed the black book from its binds and, with slow and calculated movements, opened it. The words on the first page seemed to shine in the dim light, the cursive writings in their foreign language like beautiful sketches, drawn to precision. She'd held this particular book many times, reading and rereading its contents, the lullabies of its hymns and incantations more than familiar to her.

"My child," Lenore whispered, her mind drawing up images of a past life, one where Everlore did not exist, and all had seemed right with the world. "How many times did I sing you these words? Would you remember them if I sang them to you again?"

Tears welled in her eyes, yet she smiled, knowing that time was repaying her for her patience. She flipped through the pages, singing softly to herself, feeling the words of the book take on a life of their own and soar through her body like a warm breeze. She closed the book softly and attached it to its place, running a finger across the cover once more before turning away.

Lenore's golden hair fell over her right eye like a curtain to the window of her soul. She had narrow cheek bones adorned with strands of her bright golden hair. The movement of her body was as calm yet unpredictable as the wind crooning outside. And from the quietness that glimmered in her eyes, it could be drawn that the same calmness was guiding the movement of the thoughts in her head.

She then moved past the books and back to the window she'd originally been standing at. She gazed at the skies overtaken by the piercing dark clouds, then her sight fell on the town she called her kingdom.

The town of Everlore was relatively small. Compared to the city of Calen, it was the size of the suburbs alongside a couple of neighborhoods. In her eyes, there was nothing but beauty glowing out of the houses in the town. However, the reality was quite different from how her eyes altered them.

The dim yellow glow of the building lights on the damp sidewalks and cobblestone pavements made for a bright undertone, as if from a distance the depths of hell could be seen shining through the ground. It was a dark and gloomy sight that found its way to her eyes and painted the picture of a forest of bright green and the yellow of the sun. But her eyes were as biased as her mind was. To her, there was nothing but beauty.

Lenore called herself the queen of Everlore. To its people she wasn't a tyrant. She was seen as one who sacrificed her autonomy for the good of the people of Everlore. To them it wasn't her greed that engulfed her eyes, but her benevolence that glimmered through the grey of her irises.

The town of Everlore was anything but ordinary. The nature of the people of Everlore was what gave the town its mystic sense. Though Lenore was their leader, she was rather seen as the guide of the spiritually weak. If one would observe the people from afar, they would think that Lenore had cast a spell of obedience on them. However, the spells she cast weren't on them but on the walls of every grey building that stood at every corner of the town. There was no speck of ordinary in the town; it was all engulfed in some form of magic that was nothing like the simple magic known to the people of Calen.

"Wind," she whispered, "what is your story? Why do you tell me what I already know?" She gazed down at her beloved city, and in the scented whiffs she sensed that there was an air of ordinariness that had seeped in through the forests of Everlore. In the calmness around her,

her ears caught the slight sound of movement, footsteps making their way to her chambers.

Company was coming up the stairs. She tilted her head and listened.

Wesley.

The shuffling of the heavy boots on the stairs indicated it could be no other. Wesley stood nearly seven-feet-tall, his shoulders lined diagonally to his chest in a way that made it look as if his muscles hung on his shoulders like two full moons hung in the wide night sky. Lenore smiled. He could not tread lightly on the narrow stairs. She pictured him before he came through the door.

His chin was narrow, sharp and pointed, and the edges of his cheeks were wide. His skin was almost a hued mixture of orange and bronze. His black eyes, with an iris that took up most of the area of his eyes, were unreadable—to most.

No one would argue he was a very strong man, even though his broad shoulders and masculine arms were almost always cloaked. He wore a maroon-colored cloak that draped behind him and a hood on his head that covered his bent neck and head. His movement was quite slow, and he walked around as if time was nonexistent, an illusion. He carried a long wooden stick that was a foot taller than him. In its center, a flame flickered in a cylindrical and transparent, candle-like compartment.

Lenore smiled as she heard him slam his staff on the floor, announcing his presence to her. She could almost see him eyeing the crescent moon on the outside of her door, a carving that mesmerized nearly everyone who laid eyes on it.

She waited.

A low humming sounded outside her door. Even though the rhythmic sound was soft, the depth of Wesley's voice had the door slightly shake. A soft wind blew, pulling the door open, as if the gusts had hands of their own and were welcoming the large man in. Lenore stood on the opposite side of the room, facing the dark green desk, her back to Wesley.

"Greetings, Lenore." His voice always sounded deep and raspy. It echoed when he spoke, but the echoes weren't the product of the acoustics of the room the voice reflected in, for even in the forests his voice would echo and resonate. It was a voice that demanded attention, respect.

"Greetings, Wesley," Lenore said softly. "You bear news for me?"

"Three of them," he replied.

"Hmmm, we have visitors," she murmured, "or intruders?"

"They've come from Calen," Wesley said as he walked into the room. "From the south."

"I know where it is. Our dear wind has been howling from the south for weeks now."

Wesley turned to his left and then back at the wall next to the door. He slammed his stick on the wooden floor and the cracks crawled round the perimeter of the room as the crescent moon on the red book shone bright.

When he turned towards her, she was facing him and her grey eyes pierced his. The light from the book was reflected in his eyes. She approached him, and his head leaned down and his back bent forward. His eyes hid behind the hood of his cloak and his lips trembled slightly.

"Have you greeted our very special guests, my dear Wesley?" Lenore asked as she looked up. Even though his head hung low, it was still at least two feet above her.

"Yes," he said, and his deep voice ceased its echoing. He hesitated before he said, "My queen. They're in the prison cell below."

"Wonderful," she said as a brief smile stretched her bowed lips and she clapped her hands. The wind howled as it slipped through the window again. "And did you leave the keys inside?"

He nodded. "The keys are in the cell, and the door to the labyrinth is on the verge of being opened."

Chapter 12

It seemed darker than Wesley's eyes in the prison cell.

Ryan would kick the big oaf's butt if he were here.

Atlanta shivered at the thought. She hadn't thought of Ryan in days, and the image of the last time she'd seen him came shattering back through her memory. Her heart felt different than her brain. She felt betrayed by him and at the same time... *Stop!* she told herself. *Focus on right now. Get your bearings. Figure out where you are and how to get out.* She inhaled a deep breath and gagged.

It reeked of death and centuries of decay. The scent of the dew, though physically closer to the prison cells than whatever was upstairs, didn't adorn the stench that engulfed the cell's air.

Atlanta squinted but couldn't see anything except a small light of the moon, a single ray that shone on the ground right at her feet. She couldn't tell if anyone else was in the cell with her, and was too scared to reach out into the darkness to feel around. Who knew what was in here with her. A corpse? A mangled monster? A hungry Vampire? Nothing seemed too promising.

Whose idea had it been to come here anyway? *Definitely not mine.*

Then she heard ragged breathing and nearly jumped out of her skin. Someone was here with her. Or something. It took her a moment to realize the ragged breathing was coming from her. She nearly laughed but it came out sounding more like a sob.

She glanced up at the prison cell window, a slit in an obliquely translucent sheet that allowed the light to enter in a single rectangular ray. It was so far above her, she doubted she'd be able to reach it. She tried to move her body and pain shot through every limb, making her draw in a sharp breath.

"Yeah, that won't work."

Atlanta ignored her uncle, slowly pushing herself off the cold floor, wincing in pain. Once she had herself in a sitting position, she leaned her back against the wall and tried to regulate her breathing. Something warm trickled down her shoulder, and when she felt for it she pulled her hand back immediately, scorching fire burning through her. The warm trickle was now blood on her fingertips. She let her head fall back and bit back the tears. Her shoulder hurt and—

"I told you," James said from beside her. "You're too emotional."

"Not now," Atlanta snapped.

But he did have a point.

They had made their way out of Calen with little trouble, a single sentry of Vampires their only obstacle; one Darian had quickly dispensed of with a blast of green flames. Atlanta found it odd Darian and Raul knew where the tunnels ended, but she'd argued to herself that Adelaide had probably placed sentries at every road leading into and out of Calen. The witch had the city on lockdown, with no one leaving and no one coming in.

Except the tunnels. Adelaide somehow didn't know about the tunnels. Yet.

It took them less than an hour to reach Everlore. Once they were near the town, they abandoned their bikes and decided to make their way into it through the forests. It had been Atlanta's idea, one she had thought wise since they didn't want to attract any attention. *Stupid idea.*

She hadn't expected the ambush of guards. She also hadn't expected the large man who greeted them to be so quick, so dangerous.

"Even Darian was pretty useless," James said. "Why do you think that is?"

Atlanta shook her head and winced. All she knew was that she was locked away somewhere, and she had no idea where the others were.

A rattling of chains made her head snap up. This time she ignored the pain. Through the dim light she made out a shadow in the far corner of the cell. Her first instinct was to reach for her sword, but her hand grasped only air.

Of bloomin' course. They took away my weapons.

The rattling sounded again, and she slowly pushed herself up onto her feet. She swayed a second before resting a hand against the wall to gather her wits. The light from the moon seemed to shift and the brightness in the cell increased slightly, pushing the shadows further away. Her eyes fell on a small podium in the center of the cell, the shape of a crescent moon, like the window, carved into the stone. Her eyes moved past the podium and came to rest on the silhouette hanging from the opposite wall, arms held high by chains that disappeared into the darkness behind it.

Atlanta pushed away from the wall and made her way towards the shadowy figure, slowly, making sure she stayed out of the moonlight.

"Careful," James warned from behind her.

But she didn't need to be. "I know," she told him.

Darian?

He gazed at her, his mouth opening and closing as if trying to speak, but words weren't coming out of his mouth. He rattled his chains in frustration, and in the darkness his blue eyes seemed to glow. He was hurt, probably worse than she was.

Atlanta rushed to him, reaching for the chains just as he fell to his knees. She wrapped her arms around his tight waist, trying to steady him, and a sudden scorching light pierced through her mind.

Suddenly she was in a house, surrounded by a beautiful warm light, the smell of incense in the air. She blinked repeatedly, trying to understand where she was, oblivious to her surroundings. A loud crash made her turn around quickly, and she came face to face with Adelaide.

Atlanta felt her heart skip a beat as she stared into the angry eyes of the witch. A green halo surrounded her, burning as if aflame, stretching out and recoiling as Adelaide charged forward. Atlanta raised her hands in defense but the witch passed through her, as if she weren't there.

This is a dream.

She turned around and raced after Adelaide. The witch disappeared into another room, and a sudden blast of green light burst around her. The warm light was gone, and in the darkness Atlanta watched Adelaide reach out and grab someone, a woman. There was a struggle and, as Atlanta watched in horror, the witch pulled a knife out from her cloak and stabbed the woman repeatedly, green fire burning through the room.

Atlanta withdrew from the heat.

It can't hurt me. This isn't even real.

But it didn't change the fact that the green light burned her. She fell against a wall, scurrying away from the flames, finding her way under a table where the fire couldn't reach her.

Beside her, hiding in the same small space, was a boy. He turned and looked at her, blue eyes gazing into hers. His mouth opened and a shrill scream escaped.

Atlanta jolted, falling backwards and hitting her head against the cold surface. The world around her swam in and out of focus, and she struggled to keep the darkness from enveloping her completely. She blinked several times and rolled onto her side, trying to fight through the blur, realizing that she was back in the cell.

"What did you do?"

Atlanta turned and saw Darian staring at her, his eyes wide, his mouth hanging open. Even in the darkness she could see his look of pure astonishment. His face was a mirror of the fear in his eyes, and for a moment she wondered if she was still in the dream. She blinked and focused. No, she was inside the cell and Darian's expression was scaring her.

"Wh-What?" Atlanta stammered.

"What did you do?" Darian shook the chains, jumping to his feet in renewed fury as he fought to break free.

"I didn't do anything!"

He fought against the iron clasped around his wrists. "Get me out of these," he said angrily.

Atlanta pushed to her feet and rushed forward, examining the chains. "I don't know how."

"Figure it out!" Darian hissed.

She suddenly felt keeping him chained would probably be better. She took a step back and gazed into Darian's furious blue eyes. "You saw it, too, didn't you?"

"I don't know what you're talking about."

She wasn't going to let up. "The vision. The one with Adelaide and the little boy. You saw it, too."

Darian seemed to slump, and his head dropped. "Atlanta," he started, his voice level and more in control. "I have no idea what you saw, but right now we have more serious issues at hand. The first of which is getting me out of these chains so we can find a way out of this cell."

"You haven't answered my question." Atlanta crossed her arms over her chest.

Darian huffed and shook his chains. "Because your question leads to nothing that'll help us now. How about we get out of here first, and then we'll talk about what you think you did or didn't see?"

Atlanta held his gaze, contemplating whether to let the matter drop. A part of her was curious, and a little voice in the back of her head urged her to grab him again. To try to see more of the vision before she had been so abruptly pushed out.

James cleared his throat behind her.

"Fine. I know. I know," she muttered, and moved forward, grabbing the first cuff and frowning as she tried to figure out how to open it.

"Darian?" a voice coughed from behind her.

Atlanta spun around, searching the shadows for the voice's owner.

"Raul?" Darian called out, his neck arching as he looked behind Atlanta.

"Yup," Raul replied, his voice hoarse.

"Where are you?"

"Chained," Raul replied, his anger apparent in his voice. "Apparently only one of us is free to move."

Atlanta squinted, and in the deep shadows to her left, she could barely make out Raul's outline. Suddenly, a flash of an image formed before her eyes. "The crescent," she whispered.

"What?"

She turned to Darian. "On the podium. There's a crescent. That's the key. It'll unlock—"

Chains rattled again cutting her off. "You're sure?" Raul asked.

"No. I'm not," Atlanta said. "Or maybe I am. I can't explain it. But I have this feeling..."

"Can we go on anything other than your feelings?" Raul coughed. "The last time we took suggestions from you, well, you know what happened."

Atlanta turned to Darian, who only shrugged. "My magic is useless. I can't call upon it to do us any good. I believe it's the chains."

Atlanta bit her lower lip and weighed her options. On the one hand, there was no logical reason for the podium to be there, but then again, why would their captors leave something that obvious out in the open for them to use?

I don't like this.

Still, she made her way to the podium. Slowly. Carefully. Keeping her eyes locked on the cold stone, her eyes tracing the shape of the crescent. When she was close enough to touch it, she felt an overwhelming pull come from it. As if it were urging her to do something she would inevitably regret.

"I'm not so sure about this," Atlanta whispered.

"Then we can think of something else," Darian said from the darkness.

Atlanta looked in his direction, then shook her head angrily. "No, we need to get out of here."

She reached out and rested her hand on the crescent, and in an instant a scorching fire burned through the stone and into her body. The fire raced through her, forcing her to her knees as she screamed in pain, and she tried to pull her hand back. But she couldn't. It was as if her hand was now glued to the stone.

She screamed. Again and again.

She stared at the crescent through tear-stung eyes, and through her blurred vision she saw it glow a deep amber. The glow intensified, quickly and surely, until it began to blind her, and burst out in a wave of white light.

Chapter 13

The shackles dissipated and vaporized into thin air. Darian, not expecting it and caught in what was happening to Atlanta, fell face-first onto the ground. He didn't even have time to put his hands out in front of him to catch himself. He fell with a hard thud.

A cool breeze suddenly picked up and circled the cell. The cold saturated his skin and accumulated in his bones, discharging the heat trapped inside him. It was pain and relief at the same time.

He suddenly started coughing fiercely, rolling onto his side. As he fought to catch his breath and clear his throat, he watched Raul push himself up and lean his back against the brick wall behind him. Another fit of coughs wracked his body, and he squinted. The light had been intense. The white flash still overwhelmed his vision, and the crescent on the podium burned brighter than the moon beaming right outside the prison cell.

"What happened?" Raul voiced the words in between gasps of breath.

Darian continued coughing violently, unable to respond, feeling like the light had somehow found its way down his throat and was pulling out his vocal cords. For a second he thought he'd lost his speech completely, feeling the way he had moments before when he'd first seen Atlanta and had tried talking to her but couldn't get anything out.

"I don't remember how we got here," Atlanta replied shakily. She was leaning against the podium, gasping for air as well. How could they breathe while he couldn't seem to catch his breath? "The last thing I remember was that goliath...and then nothing."

"My head still hurts," Raul said, rubbing the nape of his neck and wincing. "Under normal circumstances I'd thanking you for freeing me, Atlanta, but right now I don't know what's worse, the chains or that damn light." Raul turned to Darian. "Are you all right?"

Darian waved a hand and pushed to his feet. He swallowed and forced his diaphragm to relax. The coughing finally stopped. He cleared his throat cautiously, afraid it would come back. He could feel a burning in his eyes and imagined they were red now. He swallowed, trying to collect himself and clear the crescent moon from his vision. "I'm f-fine."

Clearly Atlanta wasn't worried. "What now?" she asked as she crossed her arms and gazed up at the window. "You guys are free but we're still imprisoned."

"We're not anything close to being trapped," Darian replied, moving around the room and taking everything in. Realizing how convenient the placement of the podium was. "If anything, we were put here just to find our way out."

Raul scoffed. "Really? Why would anyone put us in here if they wanted us to get out?"

"Some sort of twisted game?"

Atlanta snorted this time. "Someone's enjoying watching us in here." She shook her head, her blonde hair flying. "Probably that big oaf of a guard."

"You're right. Someone's watching us." Instead of looking up Darian watched her, knowing she had more questions for him. She wasn't going to let what had happened go. She wanted answers. She didn't strike him as the kind of woman who would wait for them either. He grinned, despite himself. He could appreciate that in her. What he couldn't understand was how she did what she had. It had taken him years of training to be able to reach into someone's mind and pull out a memory, let alone a memory as dark as the one she had seen. The fact that she'd done it so easily worried him.

"What makes you think we're being watched?" she asked in a whisper.

I know we are," Darian replied dryly. "I wasn't able to speak. Both Raul and I were tied and I believe he was nearly speechless, too." When Raul nodded, Darian continued. "The only light coming in was directed your way, and you were free to walk. Doesn't seem like whoever put us in here did so to trap us. They're trying to find out something." He paused for a moment and sighed, then turned to Atlanta. "I knew how to light the room. I woke up knowing it. Somehow it was integrated into my mind and I could see every little detail of the process we had to follow. I could even see you doing it before I knew you were in the same room. But I couldn't speak. My voice had been taken away by some sort of magic. When it was broken, I somehow forgot that I knew how to free us," he paused, "but you pulled it out of my mind."

Atlanta unfolded her crossed arms. "Crap! So, if some sort of magic's been used to play this game on us, then we've probably fallen right into Adelaide's trap." The intensity of the white light had decreased from what it had been moments before, and the crescent moon inside the room had grown shades darker. Her face tightened. "I'm not letting Adelaide win. Over my dead body."

"We don't know—"

"There's something written there," Raul interrupted them. Darian looked at him questioningly, and Raul gestured to the podium. Attached to it was a round brass knob, similar to those on the gates of old castles.

Raul moved towards the crescent and crouched to examine it closely. Darian could feel his friend's mind working wildly. Raul signaled to Atlanta and Darian. "Come and check this out."

Atlanta reached for the knob and Darian immediately grabbed her hand. "Patience," he said.

She gazed at him as he held her right hand. Then with her left, she grasped the knob and pulled it slightly towards her. A loud grinding sounded behind them, and they turned just as a wall pushed back and slid to their right, revealing a hallway with dim white lights. "Let's go."

This is too easy, Darian thought, but didn't want to argue with her.

He was right. They were meant to find their way out of the cell. It was surreal, and yet he could feel the spells woven so perfectly, as if the whole ordeal was the sick contraption of a twisted mind.

Atlanta moved first, and they followed her. As they walked through the dimly-lit hallway, he felt fear take over. He couldn't tell the others. And Atlanta never looked back to see if they were following. His pace slowed. He felt trapped. Not the physical prison, but the mental one that took over his thoughts. Somehow, he knew exactly what was happening. It was all perfectly orchestrated. Yet here he was, speechless and unable to let the others know—as if his body was forbidding him to share it with the others. His eyes were magnetically drawn to the center of the floor. He caught a glimpse of the single ray of moonlight streaming in, and he could see the entire process of escaping as clear as day.

Yet, everything was in a cloud a confusion.

Nothing made sense. Clear as day, and shrouded as night.

Why was Atlanta able to walk freely? Darian was sure Raul was going through the same thing he was. Atlanta was intentionally free, as if she was the one being tested, not him or Raul. Someone was trying to push Atlanta toward figuring out how to escape on her own. Tapping into his mind, accidentally or not, was a way to awaken the power inside her. Whoever had put them into the cell knew more about Atlanta and her capacity than he was comfortable with. They knew she had power within her, but also knew she was unaware of it.

How could that be?

He was dying to ask her, but still he walked silent behind her with his eyes glued to the heels of her feet.

Are they trying to capture us, or help us? Darian had no idea, but warning lights flashed inside his head, and he knew he had to be very careful from here on out. For his and Raul's sake, but especially for Atlanta.

Chapter 14

The dark corridor reeked of lobelia, a poisonous herb used by witches to soothe pain. Atlanta was unaware of how she knew the scent. She just did. It was more of a stench to her actually, one that crept through her nostrils and burned her sinuses fiercely. She forced her head to tilt down as an attempt to not inhale the warm air haunting her subconscious. The corridor absorbed enough light for her to see a few steps ahead of her, but too dark to see what lay ahead. She peered down at the cinderblock path they were walking on, and felt a strange sense of comfort deep inside her. She didn't recognize the feeling, but she imagined it was comparable to the same feeling an infant had when held by its mother.

She felt oddly...safe.

Which made no sense at all.

She recalled the images of her momentary lapse into what she could only assume was Darian's past. She wasn't entirely sure if that was what had happened, but there seemed no other logical explanation. She wanted to understand it, to know for sure, but she knew it had to wait. They had more pressing matters. For now, she had to be content with the knowledge that she had somehow pulled that memory out of his mind. The memory wasn't going to solve anything now. Or explain why she didn't feel frightened when she should be scared crapless.

Crapless? Who uses that word anymore? Sheesh, is it even a word?

A dim flickering light in the distance distracted her thoughts.

Raul noticed it, too. He paused in his gait. "You see it, too, right? It's a trap of some sort. I just know it. We can't head back, can't cut through anything. It's a trap and we've got nowhere to run. We're—"

"Shut up, Raul." Darian butted in. "It's not a trap."

"Really? After everything that's happened, you think we can just waltz up to some shining unknown things in the distance and be safe? How can you not feel the need to be cautious?" He seemed to be suddenly panicking—or completely exhausted and unable to think clearly.

"Whatever spell that could be cast upon us, could destroy our souls if we show fear," Darian mentioned as an attempt to calm Raul. "You have to approach the unknown with pure positivity and an open heart, for evil does not plague positivity."

Now he's back to Shakespeare, Atlanta thought, shaking her head.

She listened to their conversation, but ignored it. Her mind was racing, contemplating whether the scent of herbs and mold was familiar to her or not. Some aspect of her being seemed different to her at that very moment, but she couldn't pinpoint it correctly. She peered up to see the dim flickering light again, and realized it was a candle on the wall.

Why only one candle?

She stared in surprise.

Like a beacon showing us the way.

She anticipated another challenge ahead. Like how she'd figured out the crescent moon key in the prison room. She'd solved it, without James. He'd be proud of her, she knew that much. But still, it felt good. She felt a rush of power enter her nostrils, filled with the scent of lobelia and a hint of sage. It entered down her throat and collected in her joints. In each joint, starting with her shoulders, she felt a surge of energy meeting and overlapping. It slowly seeped down to her fingertips, and Atlanta raised her hands to her face to check for anything unusual.

"What's wrong?" Darian asked from beside her.

"I feel good." Atlanta replied.

"Good?"

"Seriously. I don't know how to explain it, but I feel good. Really good," she said, and grinned as she reassured Darian.

He stared at her and opened his mouth like he wanted to say something. Then closed it and shook his head as he followed along beside her.

They walked quietly and finally approached the rustic serrated candle holder on the cinderblock wall.

"It looks like a dagger." Atlanta reached up to touch it, then hesitated and lay her palm against the wall instead.

"Is this some twisted kind of dungeon?" Raul asked in an unsteady voice, clearly seeking reassurance and comfort.

"We'll figure it out. We must," Atlanta replied, determined in face and stance, not reciprocating Raul's assurance of safety.

He shrugged and continued to shakily observe the candle holder. The three comically stood around it, staring at the flame. It burned with a blue tint in its center.

Atlanta stared at the flame and then at the boys standing on either side of her. Darian's face was unreadable, but Raul couldn't seem to hide his anxiety. She felt for him. He was scared. A boy who was a man, but not much older than her. She wondered briefly what he and Darian had been through in their lives. Had they always known each other? What horrible things had they dealt with in their past? Or had they had experiences similar to hers? She sighed inwardly. It didn't matter. What mattered right now was saving Calen and getting out of this place. She gently put her hands on the shoulders of Darian and Raul and gently pushed them aside.

"What're you doing?" Darian reached to stop her. "We don't know what the flame contains. It could be charmed or, worse, cursed."

"A cursed flame? And what if we don't figure our way out? We'll just spend the rest of our days in this rat-hole?" Atlanta snapped at him.

Her anger burned in her eyes, and it took her a moment to realize she was overreacting. "Sorry," she muttered, "I just want to get outta here."

"Touché, Atlanta," Darian replied.

The look in his eyes. It's like he's scared of me or something. She held his gaze a moment before turning back to stare at the flame. There were different hues within the flame that made her mind soar. At first glance, she imagined herself free-falling and approaching large cumulus clouds. She imagined the clouds morphing their shapes and speaking to her. Suddenly, she began to choke. She felt as if she had inhaled a glass of iron-flavored water and she could not stop coughing. She felt her lungs fill with water like a fresh glass of orange juice being poured from a glass jar, the way James used to serve it to her.

She continued choking and forced her eyes open. *This is a test.* She fixated on the core of the seemingly- incessant flame before her. She tried to clear her throat and control the cough. Swallowing several times, she waved Darian back when he stepped forward to help her. "D-Don't!" she rasped. She bent forward and inhaled a long breath, then another. She straightened, then licked her fingers and pinched the flame.

The moment it went out, another glow appeared in the distance.

Raul glared at Atlanta disapprovingly. "See what you've done? Now what?"

"Follow the path. And make sure we don't do anything too stupid on the way." She returned his glare with one of her own. She swore she heard Darian snicker behind her.

As they approached the second candle, she could see halos of dark blue swirling in the air and beaming their way towards them. The hue of the candlelight was a darker blue, yet the light seemed dimmer. The dimness alternated with every step they took towards it.

As soon as they reached the candelabra, Atlanta blew it out. Another candle lit, its light reaching out to them from a turn in the path.

Raul seemed to hesitate each time the moved on, and continued looking disapprovingly at Darian and Atlanta, but they weren't focused on him. Atlanta realized that Darian was in sync with her. They mechanically moved together towards the next candle.

She had a feeling the trail of candlelight was leading them somewhere that wasn't a trap. In fact, she believed that if they were to be trapped or attacked, it would've happened before they were put in the prison cell. Deep inside she felt almost a little amused, her mind entrenched in the intricate details of the maze they were in. She couldn't help but notice how the brightness of the candle light would alter rhythmically from one place to the other, and the instantaneous shift of place of the flame. She got carried away in the seconds right after one flame would extinguish and the next would light, and she could hear the air carry the blue flames and travel to the other candle and ignite it.

They turned the corner, and Darian chuckled softly. "I see," he murmured.

This flame was not like the others. This time the shape of the flame confirmed Atlanta's thoughts that there were spells were being thrown around them and cast upon every inch of the maze. The flame was a hand that stretched from the wax of the candle and flickered the motioning of its bright blue fingers, signaling for them to approach.

Atlanta walked ahead of Darian, and Raul draped behind them. She broke into a jog and approached the hand. Without hesitating, she reached out and grasped the hand with her own. It didn't burn, neither did she feel physical fingers intertwining with her own. Instead, it felt more like a cool breeze that blew past her fingers and the flame extinguished.

There was darkness for seconds. Almost as if the mechanical trail of candlelight lagged and they were back in the black of the prison cell. After the moment of darkness two beams of light fell diagonally from both sides onto the ground, revealing a wooden chair. The color was faded and its legs were sharp and pointy.

"What now?" Raul asked in frustration as he turned and looked at Darian, then Atlanta, and then back at the chair.

"We figure it out." Atlanta shrugged. She walked towards the beams of light and the chair, and looked at the corners of the bricks. She was trying to trace the light back to the source of emission, but failed to find any physical evidence of the source. It was as if the light was shining from thin air, just slightly before the ceiling of that maze, dangling out of nothingness.

Cautious for the first time, she tentatively touched the chair. When nothing happened she tried moving it from its place, but it was fixed to the ground. She examined every side of the chair and its legs, but nothing changed in the perimeter around them. "We're supposed to figure this out."

"Figure what out?" Raul threw his hands up in exasperation. "That some psychopath is playing tricks on us?"

"No. It's a test." Atlanta wondered why she didn't feel anxious the way Raul appeared to be. Darian seemed calm, too, as he stood watching her. "We've reached the end of the maze. Behind this chair is a wall and to the left is the only remaining pathway, which leads to what appears to be a dead end. We need to figure it out." She moved her hands around the chair, trying to figure out the riddle on it.

Darian walked up to her.

She sighed deeply and stood up, looking at Darian while trying to keep her frustration composed, but her arms were crossed and a strand of her hair fell over her eyes and covered the side of her forehead. And Raul was not helping; his anxiety at that moment and ever since they had been in the maze did nothing but fuel her frustration even more. Darian, on the other hand, was calmer than the both of them. He smiled at Atlanta.

"What?" she said in frustration, trying to turn away from Darian.

Raul moved towards the chair and rested his hand on the back of it. Upon touching it, a slight sound of creaking whispered from a distance and Atlanta instantly turned to try to find where it came from.

For a moment, it felt as if they were not alone in the maze. However, just as both Darian and Atlanta looked around for the source of the sound, Raul sat on the chair and the sound of the creaking resounded through the maze. From the left side of the chair, at the end of the pathway, the wall slid open and revealed another path.

Atlanta hurried towards the newly-revealed path just as Raul stood up from the chair. The moment he lifted himself up and was no longer in contact with the seat the walls closed again, inches from Atlanta's face.

"This has got to be a joke," she puffed. She turned to Darian, who was squinting at the wall.

"One of us will have to stay behind."

"Absolutely not," Atlanta said. "We have no idea what this thing is, let alone how to get out. We've made it this far together. Someone's trying to split us up."

"Indeed," Raul said, nodding. "But there's no other way around it. We can't beat this with speed."

Atlanta slammed her fist against the wall and growled in anger. "This is absurd!"

"The question is, who stays?" Darian said, ignoring her outburst.

"I will."

They turned to Raul, who was already making his way back to the chair.

"I can't let you do that," Darian said.

"Of course you can," Raul replied. "This maze has something to do with Atlanta; I'm sure of it and you are, too. So, there's no question about her moving forward. And you're the more powerful of us both. She's going to need you."

Darian shook his head. "My magic is useless."

"But your mind isn't," Raul said, sitting down again. "It's not something to discuss. You're going. I'm staying." The wall grumbled and slid open, revealing a hallway beyond. "If anyone can figure out these puzzles, it's you."

"You don't have to do this," Atlanta said.

"Please, Atlanta," he smiled. "Just go. I'm tired. Besides, how much worse can it get?"

Atlanta looked to Darian, who only nodded and led the way into the next passage. She glanced at Raul, who gave her a quick smile, and then followed. "Thank you, Raul. We'll come back for you. I promise."

They walked past the line where the wall disappeared and heard another creaking sound, this time quicker and slightly less intense. They turned at the same time to look behind at Raul.

Except, he wasn't there. The chair, too, was gone.

All that remained were the two beams of light coming out of and fading into nothingness.

Chapter 15

"Why are you here?"

The deep, raspy voice sounded agitated. Raul hated the way it ground like stones against each other, making him shudder. He tried to focus on where the voice was coming from, his head still spinning. "Like I told you, we came seeking help," Raul said. "Who are you?"

"Wesley. You coming here was a mistake," Wesley stated. "We don't have any aid to offer."

"Why, then, have you kept us in your rotting underground cells? Why put us through your games and traps down there?" Raul asked, raising his head and forcing his eyes to focus, piercing Wesley with a look. *I'm not afraid of you.*

Raul sat, still strapped in the chair from the labyrinth, his magic useless, the bindings holding him down as if he were glued to the wood itself. Wesley had moved him to a room that was mostly dark except for a flicker of candlelight that kept the corner bristling with the dim orange color of the flames. And shadows. This place had too many shadows.

Wesley bent down, his head at the same level as Raul's. He scoffed, then stood up tall. Ignoring Raul's question, he slowly moved towards an open door to Raul's left and peered outside, as if he were expecting someone to arrive. "Your friends won't make it out of the maze."

Raul deliberately bit back his words, refusing to fall for the large man's attempt to stir up some sort of frustration or fear. "Never?" he said in a mocking tone. "They seemed to be doing quite well when I left them."

Wesley harrumphed. "It won't be happy any time soon."

Ha! He knew it! "Soon?" Raul squinted. "So, it's your plan that they find their way out eventually, isn't it?"

Wesley was still gazing outside through the open door; hearing Raul's question, he turned his focus towards Raul. "If they don't, I'll have to go down there and get them out myself." He shook his head, as if disgusted at the idea.

"Then what's the point of putting us through it?" Raul shook his head. "Why catch us, trap us, if only to set us free again?"

"We don't know you," Wesley replied. "The labyrinth is a test. We learn what we need to know about you from your reactions. We read your intentions and know your deepest fears while you are lost and trying to find a way to escape. It saves us the time of questioning."

Not a bad idea. "It sounds more like a deliberate attempt at entertainment."

"There is no entertainment in what we do." Wesley's lips turned down in a frown of disgust. "We choose not to waste time with lies."

Raul opened his mouth to respond, then closed it. Even though it seemed like Wesley believed everything he was saying, a light was shed on the nature of the people of Everlore. Something still didn't make sense. He felt that even though Wesley was confident in what he was saying, something was off. Like Wesley hadn't been told the truth. *The labyrinth? That's what he'd called it.* The place was a test. Raul didn't think it was a way to read people. The people of Everlore were looking for something. *Or someone.* Wesley wasn't the one in charge of the city; he was taking orders from someone else.

Raul heart dropped. What if Adelaide was here? What if this was a test from her? He had a gut-wrenching desire to look for signs of her in the brick walls of the room he was in, or to ask Wesley if she was the one pulling the strings; keeping him tied, and having Atlanta and Darian storming through the labyrinth. But before Raul uttered the questions that suddenly rained over his mind, Wesley almost magnetically walked towards the open door and outside into the dimly-lit hallway. For all Raul knew, Wesley had just drowned in the darkness that was outside. And after a short while of footsteps ringing behind him, there were no more sounds; he was completely alone, with only the echoes of his own thoughts to keep him company.

He couldn't stop thinking of how, at any second now, Adelaide could come walking through the door. Then he feared he wouldn't get to meet her, that she would kill him from the darkness without even looking him in the eyes.

A mixture of fury and anticipation took over when the only light in the room suddenly went out and he could see nothing but blackness around him. He decided to depend solely on his hearing to identify whoever was coming.

There was the sound of crunching, as if someone were stepping on dry leaves, followed by the echoes of footsteps approaching from afar. But before the sounds could sound closer, by the time he was trying to tell how far away they were, he felt the tingling of warm skin rubbing against his forehead. He wanted to stand up, jump out of his seat in surprise; his senses couldn't have failed him, but they had. Someone was standing right in front him, and from the tenderness of the touch he knew it was definitely not Wesley who had returned.

"You're quite warm," a female voice whispered calmly and softly from right in front of him.

"Adelaide?" he whispered, almost unable to control his tone as it disdainfully voiced the name.

The woman laughed, and Raul felt the heat rise in his cheeks. She was mocking him, and that angered him more than the possibility of dying at the hands of this witch.

"You wouldn't be alive if I were her," the woman replied.

Raul frowned. If it wasn't Adelaide, who could it be? His body was ready to face Adelaide, to let her try her worst. There was no one else. "Who are you?"

The woman laughed. "Shouldn't I be the one asking the questions? You're the one lurking in my town." She paused and Raul tried desperately to get his eyes to adjust to the darkness, but with no luck. "However, since I already know everything about you, why don't I share a bit of myself? I'm Lenore, queen of Everlore."

The queen? The thought seemed impossible.

"...And right now, I can see and hear everything that goes on inside your mind, Raul."

Was she a witch like Adelaide? Someone who trapped people without reason couldn't be good. She had—

She cut through his thoughts. "You could say I am a witch of some sort. Like Adelaide, in way, yes. Less wicked maybe," Lenore said, laughing. With her fingers hovering above Raul's head, the candle in the corner of the room was lit again.

"If you can read minds so well, then you would've known our intentions and known better than to put us in the cells," Raul hissed, fighting against his bindings, expressing his agitation at being tied.

"Dear, I hadn't read your minds yet." Lenore smiled, her eyes twinkling in the dim light. "Besides, where is the fun in that?"

With a clap of her hands, the candle went out, and Raul was suddenly immersed in complete darkness again. "Lenore?"

There was no reply. She was gone.

Chapter 16

Miles away, the dust still encircled in bright yellow waves round the towering heights of Calen. The screams had died out, only occasionally piercing the sound of the wind, the scattered few survivors being hunted by whatever lurked in the shadows.

Two figures raced through the storm, staying hidden when needed, bursting through the streets when the chance arose. They seemed to almost be wraiths, much like the monsters around them. However, there was intent in their movement, a deeper purpose that anyone who caught a glimpse of their movement would understand—if they were able to catch them.

Ryan and Marcus ran from one building to the next, moving with purpose and determination. They were supposed to be on opposite sides. One a young Shifter, the other an elder Vampire, and yet they were working together without question. In subtle yet swift movements they swept every corner of the city, and found nothing.

They did find survivors. Many of them, spread out across the city in groups, hiding. Ryan suggested recruiting, but Marcus quickly reminded him that the reason they were still alive was because they were out of Adelaide's, and her beasts', sight. Fighting the hybrids loose in the streets of Calen was suicide for any survivor, and the best they could do was not bring attention to themselves until some solution had been found.

As they searched, they didn't run into any hybrids. Rogue Vamps and Werewolves, eyes red, were compelled to attack them, but they had handled each with ease. Ryan hated to admit it, but they made a pretty good team. It made Ryan anxious: why were they not chasing them? Or were they on a more specific mission? One similar, if not the same, as their own?

They couldn't find what they were looking for—more specifically, who.

Atlanta was nowhere to be found.

For Ryan, the endless sweeping of the city seemed to take forever. It felt useless, but needed to be done. He had to find Atlanta. He had to explain... explain what? That he had no idea what had happened? That he couldn't remember? His memory, although foggy, was slowly returning. He could remember before his father's death, but the time he'd been compelled by Adelaide still resided in the shadows, prickling his consciousness second by second, slowly taking peeks into the realm of his awareness. As much as he wanted to forget, he couldn't help but push himself to try to remember. Something had happened. So much had changed, and yet the feelings inside of him remained the same.

"How did James die again?" he asked Marcus.

Marcus moved quietly along the shadows. "I've already told you."

Ten times? Twenty times? It didn't matter. He needed to know. He'd been a party to what had happened and he still had no memory of it. "Just tell me again. It's a good distraction."

"A good distraction from what?"

"From all of this!" Ryan's voice rose as he brought his hands up and motioned to everything around him. "To the city of Calen."

"You are not responsible, Ryan."

"You don't know." His voice dropped to a mumble, "I don't know."

"A hybrid killed James. It wasn't you."

"How come I don't remember?"

"It'll come back. Give it time. Right now, we need to focus on find-ing Atlanta. Where are the places she would go? Think hard. There are places you might know."

Ryan sighed. "Maybe the school?"

"We've been there, and it's too dangerous to enter. She's not there. Where else?"

"Her house, but she's not there." They approached the suburbs of Calen for the third time that night. There, the wave of dust was less in-tense and the green of the forests behind the houses hovered through the specks of earth in the air. The road they walked on was adorned with gravel and cobblestones that had fallen and cemented itself to the road from the wind.

"This is pointless," Ryan said in frustration as he kicked some of the loose cobblestones to the dry bushes across from them.

Marcus glared at him and then looked back at the road. Ryan could tell the Vampire was holding himself back from reacting to the hope-lessness in Ryan's voice. "If there was something better to do, we would be doing it," Marcus replied in a low voice.

Ryan walked on, quiet for a bit. Then he asked Marcus again, "I was there, right? I was there when James died?" He was glad the sand and grit was in the air—it was an excuse for the stinging in his eyes.

"You did not kill James."

"But Atlanta would be safe if James was still alive. He would protect her."

"Maybe someone else is protecting her."

"Like who?"

Marcus sighed loudly. "I don't know! It should be us!"

"I know. It should be us."

"We're going to find her, Ryan. James trained her well. She's smart, fast, an excellent fighter. She's a better Druid than most. She had the best teacher."

Ryan let Marcus take the lead as they moved forward. He knew Atlanta was all that and more. But what if all this had been planned? "What if Adelaide's gotten to her already?" Ryan glared up at the city, as if this was its fault. He knew it wasn't Calen's fault. It was his own. He'd done this. He was the one responsible. He kept the thought buried deep inside him, refusing to acknowledge it. "The longer we keep this up, the more I'm willing to believe that."

He suddenly stopped. His eyes widened as the inside of his head felt like there were daggers piercing through his skull. His fists balled up, and he felt a shudder race through him. A sharp breath escaped through his locked jaw.

"What is it?" Marcus asked.

Ryan didn't answer. They'd been walking aimlessly and Ryan hadn't taken note of where they were. Now, gazing at the willow tree outside Skylar's house, Adelaide's house, he felt a rush of emotions race through him. He fell to his knees, the memories rushing back like a constant attack on his being.

"Skylar. It was Skylar," Ryan whispered after gasping for air. "She's the one who compelled me. She's the one who put me under the spell. Skylar is Adelaide."

"You disappeared for a while after the attack on your house," Marcus walked up to Ryan and placed a hand on the boy's shoulder. "You went up to the mountains to regain your strength. That's what James said. Then everything changed when you got back."

Ryan looked past the tree and through the forests behind the house, then his sight shifted towards the house itself. He remembered he was never in the mountains when he took off after... after his father died. "I never left..." All he could remember were flashes of scenes of him being in that house. Skylar's home—No, Adelaide's house. "After seeing my father's body behind our house, I fought with the hybrid."

"You did?"

Ryan nodded. The memory came back to him, quick, like a physical assault. It hurt his head, and he clenched his eyes shut, trying to push the excruciating pain back. He didn't want to tell Marcus any of it, not really. He still had reservations regarding the Vampire, despite the fact that they were in this hell together. He wished Atlanta was here.

"I remember his face hidden under his hood," he said. "The rage was the worst of it. I had never felt anything like it. I usually feel myself shifting, the bones breaking and rearranging themselves, all of it. But not this time. This time I only saw the hybrid, and all the things I wanted to do to it." He turned to look at Marcus. "That monster killed my father, and all I wanted to do was rip it to shreds, tear it from limb to limb, bury my teeth in its flesh until I was crunching bone. The anger blinded me, and even though I tried to kill it that thing took me down like I was nothing. Like I was some teddy bear or something. And then it was in my head, and everything I did, everything I said, it was like someone else was doing it and I was only watching." Ryan paused. "I wasn't in the mountains like you told me; I was actually here. Right behind that door." Ryan pointed towards the door of the house. "Prisoner and compelled."

A light flickered behind one of the windows on the left side of the door.

"Did you see that?" Ryan asked as he lifted himself up and jogged towards the house. He didn't know if Marcus was following him or not as he sprinted to the front door. A memory of being dragged through the door flashed before him. He hadn't come here willingly after his father's death.

The sound of ceramic plates crashing against a wall echoed inside. The curtains where he'd seen the light, moved, as if pushed by a wind.

Someone's inside.

Ryan tilted his head. He swore he could hear, or sense, something flying or hovering, or something. Hadn't Atlanta said there were ravens? He glanced up in the air but the dust distracted him and he could see no birds.

"Silence!" Marcus commanded, grabbing Ryan by the shoulder as his eyes searched the whole perimeter of the house.

"What is it?" Ryan asked, shrugging out of Marcus's grip.

"I hear... something."

"Me, too. Plates be tossed. Someone's ticked."

"No, another sound."

Ryan frowned and listened. There was the dim humming he'd noticed before. "I thought it was... well, birds. Atlanta mentioned she'd seen ravens. I thought..."

"I've heard that sound before," Marcus said, ignoring Ryan. His eyes burned and his fangs glistened as he focused. "Hybrid." He signaled to Ryan to continue walking towards the house. Silently, they approached the door.

Ryan glanced in the window. He shook his head at Marcus. He could see nothing but the dark maroon of the curtains that fell over the glass. He turned just in time to see Marcus open the front door, the sound of creaking following. Ryan had no choice but to follow.

The house reeked of rotten eggs. *Sulfur.* And the gagging stench of dead... rats. There was barely any furniture inside, except for a black grand piano by the windows and a long couch just a few feet behind it.

Ryan tried to listen again, but could no longer hear anything suspicious. He cautiously moved towards the kitchen, his eyes briefly resting on a round grey ceramic plate on the table. He figured it must had been moved for him to have heard the sound when they were outside.

Something's not right.

There was blood on the wood floor right under him, and the smell of gasoline assaulted his nostrils.

Suddenly the humming returned, attacking his senses from all directions. He cringed, rushing out of the kitchen to Marcus who stood by the grand piano, his face scrunched, obviously just as uncomfortable as Ryan was.

"You feel it, too, don't you?" Ryan asked. When Marcus nodded, Ryan continued, "It's like someone's clawing at the inside of my head."

Marcus didn't answer.

The door leading outside creaked and then slammed shut. Marcus held up a hand, signaling for Ryan to wait. The ground beneath them began to shake. The walls vibrated. The piano played itself in and out of key until its legs collapsed and fell to the ground, ending the banal piece it was playing.

"Marcus?" Ryan shouted.

Marcus stood stoic, staring at the closed door, as if expecting something to burst through it any moment.

Ryan glanced frantically around. *What's going on?*

Then he looked up at the ceiling, trying to see what was going on outside the house, above them. *Something's falling from the sky*. A plummeting sound increased, descending at an incredibly high speed.

Suddenly, a burst of flames exploded outside the house, flashing against the dark curtains.

Ryan braced himself, the force almost throwing him off his feet as he cursed. Flames began eating the porch outside. The house groaned in protest and trembled.

"They've found us!" Ryan yelled.

"Out!" Marcus screamed at the same time. "Back door! Outside now!"

But it was too late.

The crevices of the house enlarged and the cracks on the walls distanced themselves from the pillars of the house. The shaking made progress almost impossible, and before they could find their way out of the pandemonium around them the house collapsed and fell.

Chapter 17

Fury.

It was all Marcus could feel, all he allowed himself to feel. The cold bricks and wooden foundations of the house lay around him, on top of him, crushing him. He felt none of it, though. All he could feel was a blind rage that he let encompass him completely.

This is not how I will end.

Pushed by the purest of survival instincts, Marcus pushed. He felt his bones crack and his skin rip, but he kept going, growling in anger as he heaved the stones off of himself and stood tall. The wind lapped at him, the dust encircling him as he breathed in the night air, letting his body heal.

The house lay in shambles around him, devoid of any structure, nothing more than rubble and dust. He scanned the wreckage, searching for Ryan, and when he couldn't find him, stretched and readied himself for the long search.

He'd better not be dead.

It dawned on him, then and there, that for the first time in centuries he was willing to openly admit he needed help. He shook in anger, unable to fathom how it had come to this. His kind was always called upon to assist, not be the ones seeking assistance. Yet, here he was, standing in the rubble of what was once the witch's lair, hoping his only ally was still alive somewhere beneath the heaps of stone and wood.

The sound of hissing echoed around him, and the humming began to pick up. Marcus froze, looking at the line of trees, his eyes searching the darkest of shadows. If the hybrids were still here, and he knew they were, they remained hidden.

From the midst of swirling dust, silhouettes began to take shape. Marcus waited as half a dozen men and women emerged from the dust, holding in their hands makeshift weapons of bats and crowbars.

Humans.

Marcus would have laughed if he didn't know exactly what the hybrids were attempting to do. They knew the humans would be no match for Marcus, and had probably sent them to distract him. To keep him busy while they found an opening for their own attack.

"This is absurd," Marcus whispered, taking deep breaths as he readied himself for the upcoming fight. He tried one more sweep with his eyes, hoping to find any trace of Ryan. In a situation like this, he could use the Wolf's help.

Especially since Marcus had no idea how many hybrids were actually out there. He knew Adelaide would underestimate his powers, now more than ever when he had no army to back him up, but he doubted she would be stupid enough to send just one of her puppets after him. There would be more. There had to be more.

Anything else would be an insult.

Marcus smiled as the first of the humans raced towards him, a large man with a bat, stumbling forward as he attacked. Before the man could even swing his weapon, Marcus backhanded him. The sound of breaking bones cut through the otherwise-silent night.

Where are you, you damned pup?

The others attacked and Marcus quickly tore through them, his claws and fangs ripping the flurry of flesh apart, their weapons barely making him flinch. Within minutes he was surrounded by bloody limbs and wide-eyed corpses.

"You call that a challenge?" Marcus screamed into the night. "You insult me!"

"Marcus!"

Marcus barely turned when a blur of fangs and claws raced past him and threw him off his feet. He crashed to the ground, rolling gracefully and jumping back up just as the blur made for him again. Marcus was quick, dodging and attacking at the same time, his hands wrapping around the fleshy neck of his attacker.

Marcus froze.

"Bane?"

The Vampire commander's fiery red eyes bore into his, and Marcus immediately released his hold. Bane jumped back, away from Marcus, his lips wide in a menacing smile that revealed blood-stained fangs. Marcus gazed at his old friend in disbelief, the one Vampire who was almost as old as he was. He had known Bane for centuries, trusted him with his life. Bane had always been a loyal commander, and seeing him like this, compelled, unaware of what he was doing, made Marcus furious.

How many more of those I trusted are out there, hunting for me?

"Bane, you're alive?" Marcus stared in disbelief.

The Vampire commander chuckled, a raspy coughing sound that sounded like a rabid animal that had found its evening meal. Bane crouched, watching Marcus intently, his red eyes burning.

"Bane—"

"The era of Vampires is over, Marcus," Bane hissed. "There is only Adelaide and the destruction she will bring down on this world. Yield, Marcus."

Marcus let the anger take over once more, and he clenched his fists. "Your words fall on deaf ears, Bane," he said. "Kneel. Return to your senses."

"You no longer command me," Bane snapped.

"I will always be your superior," Marcus returned. "I am your maker. Kneel!"

"You will die tonight, Marcus." Bane laughed. "And with your death will come a new age for our kind. A stronger age."

From the corner of his eye, Marcus saw movement at the tree line. From the shadows three figures stepped out into the moonlight, eyes ablaze.

Hybrids.

The humming intensified.

"Yield, Marcus," Bane hissed.

"Never."

"You will not survive the night."

"Maybe," Marcus replied. "But my death will not come at your hands."

Bane growled and sprang, his speed incredible, racing towards Marcus with fangs bared. Marcus waited, allowing his commander to come closer, before suddenly turning and lashing out. His fist connected with Bane in a sickening sound of crushed bones, and the Vampire commander was flung to the side. The force should have been enough to keep Bane down but he was on his feet in an instant, as if Marcus had merely slapped him about.

Marcus wasn't surprised, though. He had seen it several times during his fights in the city. The compelled were bolder, more vicious, oblivious to pain or threat with their blind determination. It made fighting them harder, and Marcus had realized early on that the only result of a fight was certain death. Most of the time he made the choice easily, wiping out the enemy without a thought. But Bane was different. He was a friend, and Marcus was determined to find some way other than killing him.

Ryan growled behind him, and Marcus held up his hand in protest. "No!" he shouted. "I'll handle this."

Bane laughed and came at Marcus again, this time much faster, and although Marcus was able to match the Vampire's speed, he was soon thrust off his feet and slammed to the ground in a shower of gravel and dirt.

"This is the end, Marcus," Bane spat.

Marcus kicked out, hard, and Bane rolled away only to jump back to his feet and attack again.

I can't keep doing this. I need to stop him.

But nothing kept Bane down. They slashed and tore at each other, a blurry mix of fangs and claws. Marcus tried to pin him down several times, but Bane's determination was too strong. Blind rage had taken over the Vampire commander, and there was no stopping him.

"You can't keep this up for long," Bane hissed when Marcus slammed him against a tree, the trunk cracking with the force, making them both jump out of its trajectory as it crashed to the ground.

He's right. It needs to end now.

"One last chance, Bane," Marcus said. He didn't expect Bane to listen, and when his friend charged at him again Marcus lashed out, hard and fast, his fist burying itself in the Vampire's chest.

Bane's screams of pain pierced the night like a banshee's call of the dead. He hung in the air, suspended at the end of Marcus's arm. Marcus pulled his hand back, clutching Bane's heart. Bane collapsed onto the ground, still and dead.

Marcus turned towards the hybrids, their bodies appearing and disappearing with the shifting shadows, only their eyes a sure indication of their presence.

He held Bane's heart up for them to see, then crushed it in his hand.

The sound of moving rubble came from behind him, and Marcus turned just as Ryan pushed himself out from underneath the blanket of bricks behind him. He rushed towards him, grabbed him by the arm, and pulled him to his feet.

Ryan's knees buckled, and Marcus had to wrap his arms around the boy's waist to keep him from falling.

"Brace yourself, pup," Marcus whispered.

Ryan looked at him, then followed the Vampire's gaze. Marcus could see the features on Ryan's face shift when he saw the hybrids, and underneath his hands the boy's body began to bend and change.

"Calm down!" Marcus hissed.

But it was too late. Ryan pushed him back, and Marcus watched as the boy began to shift and change, morphing into his Wolf form. The hybrids had made their way towards them, slowly, their mouths open in wide grins, ready for a fight. Marcus took a few steps away from the shifting Wolf and turned to face the oncoming attack.

"Honor your father's memory," Marcus yelled. "Avenge his death!"

With that, Ryan howled, the full moon bathing him in its silver glow, and charged forward with Marcus close behind.

Chapter 18

"Do you think they've killed him?" she whispered.

Atlanta and Darian had hurried through the labyrinth mostly in silence. Time had lost all meaning, and only the sound of their footsteps echoed in the otherwise silent corridors.

They'd barely said two words to each other. Every turn in the labyrinth provided a new obstacle, a puzzle that needed solving. Atlanta's mind that had once felt awake and ready for anything, now felt drained, and after Raul's disappearance they were on constant alert. She was exhausted, and so was Darian, their breaths coming in heavy gasps. Their silence was now a mutual understanding that they needed to save their energy for the tasks at hand rather than waste it on useless discussion. How long had they been in the catacombs under the city? Hours? Days?

Atlanta sighed and glanced at Darian. His eyes were downcast, his lips moving as if in silent prayer. She knew he was trying to figure out how to escape their predicament. This had gone on too long. And Raul...

There had to be some connection between all the tests they'd been put through. She went through everything quickly, trying to find some link. After leaving Raul behind, they'd arrived at a brick wall with a pipe dangling out of it. Water dripped down, but vanished the moment it touched the ground. On the left corner of the wall had been the stem of a flower planted right in the concrete. Darian had realized they needed to transfer the water with their hands and wash the flower with it. So they did. After minutes that felt forever of waiting, the brick wall disintegrated into red dust.

Since then, everything that came was a mystery that needed to be solved quickly. Each appeared to have more to do with the basic principles of nature than anything else. They turned off flames with sand deeply engrained in their hands, watered roses with the essence of life, ate fruits on branches of trees growing sideways from the walls of the labyrinth, and even sang to statues of birds on closed walls.

Still, it didn't seem like they were coming any closer to finding a way out.

"Do you think he's dead?" she asked again.

"If we're in one of Adelaide's games, we can't exclude that possibility," Darian replied dryly.

Atlanta hid her face from his and stared into the distance ahead of them, hoping to see an end to the confinement of the walls around them. "He might not be. Maybe this isn't Adelaide."

"Who else could it be?"

"I don't know."

"It's her." Darian sighed.

"She does tricks, not games or tests."

"How do you know?"

Atlanta shrugged. "I don't, I guess. She tricked me."

"Yeah," Darian's voice carried a tone of tiredness in it, "and this could all be a trick, too. Some sick game she's playing. Maybe she took Evermore long before Calen."

"Wouldn't you have known that? Aren't you the Coven?"

"I am," Darian said angrily. "It apparently isn't very helpful. You never heard of me."

"My Uncle James once mentioned something about the Coven, but I always pictured him to be an old man, full of knowledge and experience."

"Sometimes I feel older than I am."

Atlanta sighed. "So do I."

"My father was the Coven leader before me. He wasn't very old. But he was wise."

Atlanta was silent a few moments, not sure how to respond. "I don't know my father. He died when I was a baby." She pushed forward, not wanting to tell Darian her past. It didn't matter now. "This seems endless," Atlanta huffed in frustration.

"There's nothing else to do but move forward."

"You sound so encouraging," she said sarcastically, then bit her lip. This wasn't Darian's fault. "Sorry. I'm just not used to this."

"How so?"

"Give me something to punch." She slammed her fist into her other hand. "That's where I shine."

Darian chuckled. "A lot of those puzzles, you solved."

"I never said I was stupid." Atlanta laughed, for the first time in hours. "I'm just out of my element."

They turned another corner, and Atlanta hit the wall with her fist. "Seriously?!"

"What is this?" Darian asked at the same time.

In front of them was a wall unlike any of the others they'd come across. It was about twenty feet high and about twice as wide. The wall wasn't made of stone or bricks, but a series of tree branches perfectly woven with one another so as to leave little or no gaps between them, like a web of chestnut brown hairs tangled into a perfect tapestry.

"What's that?" Atlanta pointed to the ground by the center of the wall.

A black box sat, its lid adorned with a ruby stone.

"What now?" Darian exclaimed in frustration, raising his arms in the air and turning his back to the wall. It was clear he had reached the end of his patience.

Atlanta walked to the wall and crouched down to examine the box. She cautiously lifted it, and glanced around to see if a wall opened or something happened. Nothing. Carefully, she tried opening it, but couldn't. Using her strength, she tried harder. "It's locked. Almost as if someone glued it tight." She frowned, rolling the box over in her hands, feeling its sleek surface, trying to figure it out. There was nothing out of place or anything that needed to be rearranged or moved.

She looked up at Darian, but he didn't seem interested in what she was doing. She watched him wiggle his fingers, his lips moving, as if he was trying to will his magic back.

"A little help here," she called to him.

Darian scowled and then looked at her. "What is it?"

"*I'm* trying to figure this out," she replied hotly, her nerves frayed as well. "Sorry to disrupt your magic-mojo-mumble. One of us is trying to get us out. Maybe once we're outside this crap-hole, your magic'll come back. Maybe you could take a moment and help me open this box. If it's not too much."

"Magic what? You think only one of us is trying to get us out of here?" He didn't try to hide his frustration either. He rolled his eyes at her, not offering to help with the box as he moved in circles back and forth. Every time he turned his eyes towards the tree-wall, he clasped his hands as if he were about to pierce through it with his fists. "You're not the only one feeling trapped here, Atlanta. You think you know it all—" He was sweating, his forehead glistening.

"I don't think I know it all! Not once have I ever said that! You're the one who came looking for me. I didn't ask for your help—you know what, forget it! Maybe you should've sat in the chair instead of Raul." She stood up and brushed her hands on the branches of the tree, trying to uncover a spot that felt different or odd. "I'll figure it out myself," she mumbled. Nothing looked like a test of any kind here. Just a big stupid pile of branches and a box. What were they supposed to do? Scale the vine wall? And then what? *Come on!*

Darian suddenly spun around and stomped over by her, swiping the box off the floor. He frantically tried to open it, but all his efforts proved to be worthless. "Damn it, open!" he screamed.

Even though his anger had gotten the best of him and he'd lost complete control, it was as if it was all calculated and preset. A loud click echoed in the labyrinth corridor, and the lid of the box ascended and floated on top of the box.

Atlanta raced to his side and looked inside. Empty. After all that? "How'd you do that?"

"I don't know." He shrugged, his anger evaporating. "I literally just yelled at it to open."

When the two fell into silence and tried to look for something inside the box, it closed once more.

"Open," Atlanta shouted at it.

The box opened once more on its own, and the lid hovered above it then fell back when the silence took over.

"So it opens when we ask it to, and closes when we don't say anything." She glanced underneath it. Not that she expected to find anything there.

"Still nothing inside of it. How bloody helpful!" Darian snorted.

The box opened once more.

"Not much of a smart box. Seems it just reacts to anything spoken," he said.

Atlanta moved away from the box, trying to see if anything would change with the vines when the box was open. Nothing. After a while of straining, she gave up on trying to figure it out. Fatigue set in. She leaned her back on the wall and sat next to the box. She wished James was here. He'd know exactly what to do. Better than pacing Darian. Who never seemed to sit still. *Kind of like you?* She almost imagined

James saying that to her. "You're making me uneasy with all the moving around," Atlanta snapped.

"Yes, because you're the embodiment of calmness," Darian retorted. "Didn't you just say you wanted something to punch?"

You? "That's not helping," she replied, glaring at him. She turned away and buried her face in her knees.

Darian's frantic moving around ceased, and he let out an audible sigh. He sat down next to her on the other side of the box. The clasp of his fingers on his palms began to ease and his fingers tore themselves free from the grip of his fists. "I'm sorry I'm not much help," Darian said softly.

"It's fine," Atlanta replied, looking up. "I...I'm not much help either. Sorry about what I said about wishing you and Raul traded places."

"I'm sorry I snapped."

She snorted, and tried to smile. "Yeah, you don't seem the kind of person who usually gets all riled up."

"You know, I used to be very calm. All the time. I never had a problem with my own feelings."

"What changed?" Atlanta asked. "This prison?"

The box remained open, the top hovering over them, the ruby in its center glistening.

"Before here." He sat quiet, staring vacantly at the box. "I can't believe I'm telling you this," he said as he briefly smiled. "I didn't mean specifically you. I just mean that I've never told anyone this."

"Told me what?"

"I had to kill someone I loved."

Atlanta frowned.

"Her name was Serena," Darian continued, his eyes closing briefly.

The ruby began glowing brighter, spreading a red hue over the ceiling that went unnoticed by them both.

"Why'd you kill her?"

"She was a Werewolf and I, I was just one of the agents of the Coven, undercover in a university in Spain where we met. It was like a fairytale. She completed me, made me feel like I didn't have to continue living the life I did. She made me feel like we could somehow have a future together."

"You were in love..." Atlanta whispered, wondering briefly where Ryan was. *Not that I love him. He was with S—Adelaide. He might still be, for all I know.* She focused on Darian, pushing the thought away. It was too painful.

"But eventually we realized that, to have a life together, we had to somehow both escape the things that kept us prisoners. Me the Coven, and her the pack. I should've never told her about how much I wanted to be free of having to always be in danger, she shouldn't have had that in her heart. It was all because of me... and I had to correct my mistake."

His voice shook, and Atlanta felt an urge to reach out and hold his hand. "What happened?"

"One full moon, a Wolf from Serena's pack killed a Vampire. The Vampires in the town weren't many, but they became angry. They attacked the pack and the Werewolves easily overthrew them. But that didn't stop them. The Werewolves were high on the power the full moon gave them. They believed they were unstoppable. Serena led them towards a base of ours on the outskirts of the town. They attacked the agents of the Coven there. As soon as I heard, I rushed to the base..." He closed his eyes. "The base was on fire. The moment I saw the Werewolves recklessly turning everything that came their way into ashes, I knew I had to stop them." He sighed and opened his eyes. "I knew she was doing it to set me free. And although she was trying to save me from misery, she attacked me. She'd lost control. She couldn't stop herself. The last time I looked into her eyes I had my blade in her heart, her blood all over me." Darian lowered his head, and a sudden silence fell over them.

"I'm so sorry," Atlanta whispered. She thought about Ryan again. Could he have been out of control, too?

"Don't be," he answered. "Ever since then, I've been losing control of my emotions. My mind and heart found different paths, opposite to one another, in a constant struggle."

"Don't blame yourself," she said, trying to console him. "It won't bring her back, and it'll never make you feel any different, just worse maybe."

"I started hating myself after that. All the love I had for her turned into hatred the moment I killed her. That hate I directed at myself."

I get it. She wanted to comfort him, to let him know that he wasn't alone in his struggle, that she blamed herself for her uncle's death and everything that was happening in Calen. But he knew that; he had, after all, tried to calm her earlier, back in the remains of her home, when everything seemed dark and lost. She had no idea he was struggling with his own demons.

The lid of the box fell back into place and the ruby ceased shining.

"You know, since you told me this, I feel like I'm obliged to share something with you, too," she said.

"You don't have to."

"I know, but I want to," Atlanta nodded. "Consider it a show-and-tell session of dark secrets and bottled emotions."

Darian chuckled. "Very well, be my guest. Bestow upon me your sorrows. For I am the Coven. It is my job to listen. Misery loves company."

"Poetic," Atlanta snickered.

"Shut up and talk."

"I prefer you talking like that than some Hand of the Coven." She grinned and it slowly died on her lips. "I used to hate myself, too," Atlanta began in a serious tone, "but for different reasons. Ever since I was young I felt helpless and weak. So weak that I would do the most reckless things to prove to myself that I was stronger than I believed."

"I think I can relate to that," Darian said. "What kind of stupid stuff did you do?"

"Like trying to jump out the window of my room to prove my legs could withstand the distance." When Darian gave her a look with one eyebrow raised she laughed. "And then I ended up with a broken leg instead, and scars on my arms." She leaned over and pulled up the sleeve of her suit, showing him a scar on her right arm that started at her wrist and ended right above her elbow.

They both laughed quietly and glanced at the top of the box as it floated above them, noticing the red glow of the ruby for the first time. Neither said anything about it, though.

Atlanta stared, as if mesmerized by a flickering fire. "The thing is, I had to find out where the weakness stemmed from. The moment I knew it and understood, it was easier for me to stop hating myself so fiercely." Her gaze dropped down to her hands and she picked absently at the dirt that wasn't there. "But it was just the anger that went away. The hatred remained."

"Where did it start?" he asked.

"The moment my Uncle James told me that my parents died in a fire when I was five. I was twelve when he told me, and I felt a tingling right under my chest. I felt that there were flames setting fire to my insides and leaving me dry."

"I'm sorry," he whispered softly and put a hand on hers. "I didn't know your parents died when you were young."

"It's okay; time heals all wounds, right? That's what they say. Or at least I think about it less nowadays. When I found out what had actually happened to them I started training with Uncle James, trying hard to stop the fire inside me. I avoided facing the sadness and grief, and instead turned it into anger to make myself feel stronger than the pain I didn't want to face." She shrugged. "But it never helped pacify the feelings eating me alive. Worse, it was fuel to the fire growing inside me; it did nothing but make me angrier." She'd tried to hide it. But always knew it was simmering inside of her. She wondered if James had known, too.

"Anger feeds on anger," Darian said. "Only peace can disintegrate it."

"Thing is, I didn't want to believe that, because I didn't want to make peace with the fact that my parents were never coming back. I had thought they were somewhere out there, trying to make the world a better place so that I could grow up happy in it. I always hoped I'd meet them someday."

The red light from the ruby shifted and now fell on the wall behind them. It shone brighter than before and spread throughout the hall.

"You see what I'm seeing?" Darian asked quietly as the red waves of light fell under their feet like bright colored shadows.

She nodded and continued talking, as if drawn to the light. Almost thinking her confession was helping move the ruby and create the light. "I just wish I could meet my parents, see what everyone sees when they compare their faces to their parents' faces. Believe in love, or disbelieve it, because of seeing how my parents love, or hate, each other. I don't know, whatever there is in that world of families, I wish I could take a peek at it, be embraced by it." She paused a moment, realizing she'd been talking a lot. She turned her gazed to his face. Darian's eyes glistened with what seemed to be hidden tears. She'd been so carried away by her own thoughts, she didn't realize he was still holding her hand. A sense of fear took over her heart, because at that moment she felt something that was bittersweet. She slipped her hand from his and turned to stare in front of her. "It's childish, I know. I just wish I could see my mom and dad." She sighed.

Suddenly, the branches of the trees behind them began unfolding and slipping away. The light from the Ruby engulfed the room completely and the bottom part of the box began glowing.

"What's going on?" Darian whispered.

"I don't know," Atlanta whispered back.

They stood and stared at the walls as they opened. The tree branches fell to the floor and turned to dust, revealing a bright white light from beyond the wall shining on them. There was a shadow in the distance.

Atlanta squinted, making out the figure of a woman with long hair.

Darian stood still beside her. "Careful, Atlanta," he whispered.

She gave a curt nod. She didn't know who to expect, but knew that they'd finally found their way out of the labyrinth. Her heart sped, as she feared it was Adelaide.

The woman slowly drew closer and Atlanta let out a breath she didn't realize she'd been holding. It wasn't Adelaide. The woman's eyes were blue.

"Who is she?" Atlanta whispered, reaching for Darian's hand.

Chapter 19

"What have you found?" Adelaide's green eyes glowed as Michael appeared before her, his hood falling from his head, the sound of ravens above signaling the return of the scouting party.

"It's exactly like you said." Michael smiled. "She's there."

Atlanta.

The name left a bitter taste in her mouth. Ever since she'd learned of the girl's escape from Calen, with two strangers no one had ever seen before, she knew Everlore would be their destination. It was the only thing that made sense, the only place the little blonde could possibly find anyone strong enough to help her.

James trained you well, young Skolar.

"How far has she gotten?" Adelaide asked.

"The ravens saw her walk out of the labyrinth. She's been able to get past Lenore's first challenge."

Adelaide laughed. Oh, how she wanted to be there when Atlanta came face to face with the witch. "It seems luck is on our side, my pet," she said. "The last Skolar, and the books of magic as well. This'll be a fine day for us all."

Michael snickered and fell to his knees beside Adelaide. "I smell blood," he hissed. "Lots of it. It's making me hungry."

"In time, my pet, in time." Adelaide took in a deep breath and gazed at the city in the distance, the magical walls surrounding it mirroring the forests. "Gather the others."

Michael raced to the task, and Adelaide walked to the edge of the tree line. "Oh, how I have missed Everlore," she whispered, chuckling. Movement in the forest behind her let her know that her hybrids were ready, and with a wide smile on her face she led the way.

She floated just inches above the ground, surrounded by a dark green glow as she moved. She held a book in her hands that had fragments of dust carved into its cover, like stains that bled through the pages so much that they took it to be home.

Michael was like a shadow, alternating between racing ahead of her and behind her, like two chess pieces on a board. His presence calmed her, her little pet, a being so beautiful and dangerous he would die before anything were to happen to her. Even with an army of hybrids at her back, she rarely felt at ease without Michael by her side.

Adelaide looked over her shoulder at the dozens of hybrids following her. Ever since Atlanta opened the door, they had multiplied. The hybrids were made so that, with every full moon, Adelaide could create another hybrid from the blood of two others. With about dozen of them set free from behind the door of the Dome, their multiplying was ceaseless. Soon she would have an army so great, nothing could stand in her way.

"We should have killed her when we she was within our reach," Michael spoke, his voice a dark monotone beside her.

"My dear boy, this little brain I gave you thinks only of killing and controlling. You have no idea what we are getting," Adelaide responded, her lips stretching and a slight laugh lingering in her chest.

Her eyes were set towards the distance. Her mind saw nothing but red, black, and grey hues that she sought to set her eyes upon. Centuries of longing were turning into a movement in her chest that was so rhythmic, it could be mistaken for heartbeats.

"Can't you see what we did in Calen was nothing but an opening for the path to find our way here?" she continued.

She traced a finger across the leather bindings of the book in her hands. It had also been locked away in the Dome along with her hybrids, and ever since she had laid hands on it she rarely let it out of her sight. It was no book of teaching, nor was it a book of spells. It was an inkless book that, when possessed by a witch, ultimately allowed her control over any witch whose eyes glowed the color of the book's green cover. It made her capable of controlling all the witches who had helped her in the time of the insurgence.

The sky was dimming and the light of the sun created a dim blue canvas for the streaks of red from its paintbrush of light. The croaks of the ravens were suddenly silenced as the walls of Everlore appeared in the distance ahead.

She knew that even if the inhabitants of Everlore knew of her coming, they wouldn't be able to stop her. Their use of the power of natural forces wouldn't stop the dozens of heartless hybrids and the power of her spells. And even if the hybrids were to be stopped they would divert everyone, and Adelaide would be able to enter the town and get what she came for.

"We should have finished her. It would've been so easy," Michael whined.

"We couldn't have killed Atlanta," she whispered to Michael. "She was needed. To lead us to where the powers we need is. Like a sheep to the slaughter, she has led our army exactly where it needs to go."

The wind howled as they neared the dark grey walls of Everlore. From deep within the town, the trees shook and the leaves fell on every doorstep. A warning for all to be ready for an oncoming evil. Adelaide smiled as she watched her hybrids prepare themselves for the onslaught, their breathing heavier in anticipation of the havoc they would wreak. Michael raced between the ranks, hissing out her orders.

The wind echoed through windows and the crevices of every house in Everlore. From above, the gargoyles glided across the sky, darkening it as they hovered above the houses. Black hail fell from their jaws, hissing as they touched the surface of the walls and melted them down. Everlore's greatest defense fell quickly.

The ravens stood on the remains of the walls as a sign that darkness had arrived, as if the dissipation of the walls weren't enough. The hybrids hovered into the town and the silence fled away into endless thrumming. Adelaide followed, and with a slight nod they raced down the streets in a blur.

The first screams sounded almost immediately, and in the distance a burst of fire erupted with a thundering explosion. *This is going to be beautiful,* Adelaide mused. A tall woman raced out into the streets, then turned around, blue fire raging from her hands. The flames burst out in a jet towards one of the houses, and before she could turn around one of the hybrids was on her, tearing at her flesh. Her screams were cut short as blood spurted out of her.

More blue fire erupted to Adelaide's right, followed by the hissing of her hybrids and the screams of the dying. She floated down the road, Michael close to her side, making her way deeper into Everlore. Every now and then she'd let her own green fire burst out, and watch in manic laughter as a house burst into raging flames.

From between two houses a trio of men ran into the street, turning to face her, blocking her way. The larger of the men held a staff that burned blue.

"Wesley," Adelaide greeted, smiling. "I was wondering when you'd show up."

From either side of the trio hybrids appeared from between the flames, hissing, fangs bared, ready to attack. Wesley held his ground.

"This stops now, Adelaide," Wesley said, pointing his staff at her.

Adelaide laughed, throwing her head back. In the distance, she could see the watchtower. She turned to Michael and nodded.

"Burn it all, and find me up there," she commanded.

Michael let out a loud growl, and the hybrids attacked just as Adelaide disappeared.

Chapter 20

"Who *are* you?" Atlanta had stepped in front of Darian, as if to protect him, her hand lingering dangerously close to the dagger in her belt. Inside, a small voice shouted in warning, letting her know that their journey had not yet ended. That their escape from the labyrinth did not necessarily mean they were safe.

I know her. The thought hit her like a sudden revelation, her brain straining under the force of trying to place the woman's face. *I think.* She felt Darian's hand on her arm, as if reassuring her, and she drew strength from the touch.

"I'm Lenore," the woman said, "and I'm very pleased to see you."

"Yeah, you throw one heck of a welcome party," Atlanta shot back.

Lenore laughed. "I see you have your uncle's sense of humor."

Atlanta froze. "How do you know my uncle?"

"I know a lot about you, Atlanta Skolar," Lenore said. "More than you think."

"I know nothing about you," Atlanta replied tightly. *Except that you like to trap people and play games.* "So you have me at a bit of a disadvantage here." Atlanta's hand tightened around the hilt of her dagger.

"That's true," Lenore said, smiling. "But all will be clear soon." She looked back and forth between the two of them. "I never thought I'd see you both again, let alone hand in hand."

"Again?" Darian's voice broke in anger. "What do you mean, *again*?"

"Yes, again, my dear boy," Lenore replied, unfazed by Darian's outburst, "That, unfortunately, is a question to be answered later. I've been waiting for this moment for years." Lenore took a few steps until she was standing right in front of them.

Atlanta's hand tightened and began to pull her dagger out, when something suddenly made her stop. She was speechless, but at the same time her mind was racing. Something about Lenore made her fears subside, as if staring into her eyes made everything better. Like Lenore could stop Adelaide. Bring James back. Fix everything.

But that was impossible.

I know you. How do I know you?

She searched her memory for a sign, any conversation with James that might have brought up Lenore's name. A picture, even. Anything. But no matter how hard she tried, the answer remained just out of reach.

"It's nice to meet you. We're sorry you've been waiting so, uh, long. But we're getting out of here," Darian said, his grasp on Atlanta's arm tightening. He began pushing past Lenore, and just before he stepped into the stream of light gushing into the corridor he bumped into a stiffness of the air. It glowed green.

"I didn't wait all this time for you to walk away now," Lenore whispered, her words drowning in a tone of mockery and playfulness. "I haven't said what you need to hear."

"You have nothing we need to hear." Darian glared at her. "Is that why you had us locked in that labyrinth?"

Atlanta felt his frustration. "Where's Raul?"

Lenore held up a hand to silence them. "Relax, your friend is safe. He's not a prisoner here, and neither are you."

"And yet you won't let us leave," Darian said, at the same time Atlanta said, "That labyrinth of yours says otherwise."

"That labyrinth was a test." Lenore shrugged. "Each puzzle you solved was there for a reason. You were forced to work together, to use brains over brute force and magic."

"You tampered with my magic," Darian said, more as a statement than a question.

"Everlore tampered with your magic," Lenore replied. "People do not know of us, of this city. It exists merely in the minds and hearts of its inhabitants, and those foolish enough to seek it out. It is but a fragment of time and space which, if not known, cannot be seen." She paused and gazed deep into Atlanta's eyes. "You know of it because of your uncle, and because of your connection to it."

"My connection?" Atlanta asked.

"Stop," Darian cut in. "You're playing with us. If we're not prisoners, let us go. Let my friend go. It was a mistake coming here."

"On the contrary," Lenore said. Her face turned into an expressionless canvas. She frowned for a moment, then turned back to Atlanta and smiled once more. "You came here to try to save your city, and I can help you. But first you have to follow me." She turned her back to them and walked past the green glow of the invisible wall.

Darian turned towards Atlanta and squeezed her hand. She looked at him and, in silence, nodded. There was no choice. They followed cautiously and glanced at each other as they passed through the green glow onto the brightly-lit path.

The ground was a series of cobblestones colored green and blue, with red stones scattered in between. The stones glowed bright red whenever they came near them. They almost looked like rubies, and the intensity of their glow was blinding.

Lenore was taking graceful, soft steps, walking in front of them. Her neck and back were straight and her dress glistened with white sparkles as it draped behind her, leading their way to follow her.

Atlanta watched her carefully, unable to tear her eyes away from the woman. *I know you.*

The words circled in her head, over and over, but try as she might she still couldn't find an answer. A part of her wanted to ask Lenore straight out, to put her confusion at ease, but something told her that the woman wouldn't be quick with answers.

"It's a shame you both don't recognize me," Lenore said in a soft tone. "Especially you, Darian." She turned to face them, and her blue eyes seemed to glisten in the sunlight.

Atlanta looked at Darian, the deep frown on his face, and knew that he was trying to place Lenore as well. She could almost feel his mind at work, and just as she was about to ask him he stopped.

You recognize her, she wanted to shout, a spark of envy racing through her. She turned back to Lenore, watching as the woman's eyes fixated on Darian and her smile widened.

Darian shuddered and Atlanta pressed her hand in his, squeezing to get his attention.

And suddenly it all made sense.

A rush of images flashed through Atlanta's mind. Just as before, she was pulled out of her body, out of her current setting, and thrust into a world she barely recognized. She was back in the hut, surrounded by Darian's memories, crawling underneath the table once more as she watched Adelaide make her attack.

She gazed at the young boy hiding under the table beside her, Darian's blue eyes staring back at her yet not fully taking her in. She reached out to touch him, to comfort him, but her arms wouldn't move. Darian's head turned back to the scene before him, and Atlanta did the same.

She watched in horror as green flames licked at the walls around them, the struggle between Adelaide and the woman Atlanta knew to be Darian's mother. She sat helplessly as Adelaide lifted the dagger and struck, and flinched when Darian began to scream. She was about to rush to him, to take him into her arms, when her eyes caught the face of the dying woman.

Bright blue eyes looked in her direction. There was no mistaking them.

Lenore.

Chapter 21

Darian felt numb.

How could he forget the face that faded into a sky full of dim pigments of red and blue in the night that haunted his childhood memories? The irony was that the memory had never left him. The memory of the scene of his mother being killed by Adelaide had always been the fuel for the fire that had been raging within him for as long as he remembered.

Although the memories never left him, and had always found their way to settle behind the curtains of his mind, the face of his mother and the face of Adelaide both remained a blur. A blur that kept melting into darker colors up until that very moment after he left the labyrinth. For then and only then did the blur begin to sharpen, and the truth unfold before his weary eyes.

Even his feelings didn't know whether to crumble and fall from the mountains of sorrow and anger that they had risen above, or to ride with the winds and find a higher peak of a sturdier mountain. The blood rushing through his narrow veins gushed to his brain, and his nerves cast their spells over his bones.

He felt Atlanta grab him by the arm just as his knees threatened to buckle underneath him. He could only assume she had figured out the truth like he did. He had felt her touch, had felt the soar of energy racing through him, delicate fingers scraping at his mind and reliving the memories with him. He could hear her breathing heavily beside him, just as shaken as he was, and although he wanted to turn and look at her, to find some comfort in her gaze, he couldn't. All he could see was the memory, and the tall figure of his mother standing before him.

You died, he wanted to scream. *I watched you die!*

Lenore had started walking up a set of stairs. The ruby-adorned cobblestone path behind Darian and Atlanta suddenly shut together by another tree-wall that intertwined its branches behind their backs, leaving them with only one direction to follow. Darian could feel the branches against his back, stopping his retreat. He felt them prod him forward, as if guiding him to where they knew he did not want to go. His hand tightened around Atlanta's, and he fought desperately to stop his body from shaking.

Mother.

A rush of emotions burst through him, a kaleidoscope of raw feelings that threatened to burst and engulf him. He wanted to scream and cry and laugh and shout, all at the same time. For the first time in a long time he was no longer the leader he had built himself up to become, but a mere boy hiding under a table while his mother was murdered.

Darian knew that the veil taken off his blurred mind was just the beginning of what was yet to unfold. He could sense the secrets that Lenore had yet to share, the wealth of information she would bombard him with, relentlessly, and he feared what it would do to him. And like a mystic sky obscured by clouds, the dawn of his past needed nothing but time to begin flirting with his consciousness.

What else? What else are you going to show me?

Darian's eyes were closed, his face wrinkled as his mind worked in overdrive, burning inside his skull. The curtains of his eyelids were drawn above the paleness of his ocean-blue eyes, and they fell right on Lenore's identical eyes as she climbed the stairway and pierced his stare with her smile and gaze.

The wind blew fiercely through the window, and the flames that rode the candles on the stairway flickered and danced. The warnings were blowing into Everlore, yet the reception of the signs that came from the outside was blocked by the endless rambling in Lenore's thoughts.

"You were dead," Darian blurted as his voice crumbled. "This can't be true; you're playing with my memories." He opened his eyes, rage burning within them. "Cast your spells elsewhere, witch!"

"Oh, Darian." Lenore shook her head. "What's getting into you? Why deny? I'm only sharpening the blurred images that already cower in the corners of your mind."

"You can't be here," he whispered. He projected a wall of disbelief into a screen of angry words, but on the inside the pieces were all coming together. He remembered the portraits of his mother that hung on the walls in their house in Lisbon. He criticized himself for never fixing the face in the paintings with the blur of the face in the memory of his mother's murder. Yet he couldn't take that memory for granted; the agony of every moment in that memory was a pillar of what built him. His emotions and beliefs were all just pillars mounted in the ground woven by the pain of his mother's death. And if that was untrue, if Lenore was his mother, then the whole of him needed to be scattered and carefully put back in place.

"All these years, all the pain you put me through," he caught his breath as he thought of his father and the sadness that had never left his eyes, "and you come now without the slightest shame or guilt. Grinning and flashing your existence in my face as if it's the truth." Darian's words were like a knife cutting through the air, and he could see a spark of pain etch its way onto Lenore's face. "Even if you are my mother, you're only so by name. My mother died. She was killed by Adelaide. She's the woman I'm seeking revenge for." His voice resounded and rode the flames of the candles, bristling the howl of the wind outside.

Darian shook Atlanta's hand from his and stormed up the stairs. Atlanta ran after him.

"The memories you have of me being killed by Adelaide aren't false, my son," Lenore said in whispers as she stood by the door at the top of the stairway.

Darian's momentum ceased halfway up the stairs and he fell on his knees. He felt his mind wander again through the holes of induced visions that she cast.

"I was cast to a netherworld in the west that I turned into the beautiful paradise you see outside." Lenore turned her head towards the windows that showed a vastness of green, shadowed by the grey walls of Everlore. "She stole a book that I was enslaved by, and so I became enslaved to her. But with the help of Marcus, and the elder Vampires, we were able to get the book back from her. Then she fled to another netherworld."

Darian felt he was drowning in a gloom of uncertainty. Yet, in the midst of it all, he saw what he had previously failed to see. He saw himself in Lenore. He realized the purpose behind the visions that were awoken when Atlanta had touched him. Lenore had meant for all this to happen, and everything had been set so he would understand the truth. "Mother?"

Lenore opened a door to a dimly-lit room. As Darian stepped through the door, the far wall caught his attention. Three books glowed on a shelf. Their red, black, and grey bindings on the side of the wall flashed, caught by the rays of the full moon's soft light through the windows, as if it too was drawn to the books. Darian couldn't tell what time it was anymore. It was as if morning and night had somehow become one in Everlore.

"I'm fascinated by your silence." Lenore stood in the middle of the room. "I know that words may not be enough. Pictures could be worth thousands of words, and dreams worth eternities." She raised her arms and her eyes closed. The wind was blowing, but not from the windows;

it was rather seeping through the pores of her skin and flooding the room. A beam of white light engulfed the room, and the only color breaking the whiteness was the blue of Lenore's eyes as they opened and fell on Darian and Atlanta. "I owe you both more than a dream; I owe you eternities of them. And there is nothing better than a conscious dream to enlighten you," Lenore whispered softly as the whiteness of her skin beamed ruby-red. "My son and daughter, brother and sister before me. Glide through this sky of truth and back to the moments that have for too long been obscured and hidden from you both."

The white light engulfed them, pierced their skin and warped their minds. Darian froze in his place; beside him, Atlanta shook and fell to her knees. Her thoughts and feelings rushed through him. It was as if they were one, a sudden burst of epiphany coursing through them both, binding them to each other.

Brother? Daughter?

He could hear Atlanta's thoughts as clearly as if they were his own. Upon hearing the word daughter, a word she hadn't heard in a lifetime, her heart crumbled and melted into the heart of a newborn baby, wailing in disbelief at the world that their eyes were waking to. Voids within her began filling with an alien feeling of belonging.

Atlanta looked at Darian, and he could see in her eyes that sense of familiarity. He could see she wanted to deny it just because it was in her nature to deny before examining and looking for the truth, but she couldn't. She could not deny that the moment her eyes met Darian's, all as the words son, daughter, and brother were ringing in her head, she felt that the truth had been lavished upon her by some white light. And more was still to come.

Darian's anger had ceased and the flames were mollified by the feelings coursing through him. He remembered the first time he saw Atlanta at the Dome. Emotions had gushed up and filled his mind, and had fallen like rain on his heart. He had confused the feeling with ro-

mantic admiration, yet something in him had told him that it was absurd to conclude the feeling as such.

But it all made sense now.

He knew that the heart was a compass beyond comprehension.

He knew that his heart understood what he couldn't make sense of,
that he and Atlanta were bound together, more than the simple connection between two people who had just met.

The world blackened and a single speck of light roamed around
them. The blue speck of light was like a small balloon that grew larger,
and inside it was a story to be unveiled before their eyes. Lenore's voice
began to echo from every direction, through the veil of white, under
the sky of black, and in the valleys of Darian and Atlanta's minds.

Chapter 22

*M*other?

The word echoed in Atlanta's head, filling her mind with images she didn't know. *I don't have a mother. She died. So did my father.* All around her the white light flashed against her pupils; dim shapes of moving objects slowly took form. A hand grasped hers, and she didn't need to look to know it was Darian. His presence comforted her, and although she still couldn't grasp the concept that they were related she held his hand tight.

Lenore's voice somehow sounded far away and at the same time a whisper in her ear. The dark images took form and Atlanta gazed at the scene unfolding before her, the colors bright against the white canvas behind it.

"I remember like it was yesterday, and in a way, it could be. Time has no meaning in Everlore, and memories take many shapes and forms. All convolutes into one, yet remains dispersed all the same. But nothing will change my memories of a happier time, a peaceful time, one when I was young and naïve, and believed all was good in the world."

The image shifted and changed, bringing with it the scene of waves crashing against a sandy beach. A little boy prancing in the sand, bending down, splashing in the water, gleefully dancing in the sun. His blue eyes were unmistakable. Atlanta could feel Darian's hand tighten around hers.

"Darian, my son. How bright your big blue eyes were, and still are. You had a smile that could brighten anyone's day. You'd be sitting by the beach, eyeing the ocean as if it were a canvas. Since the day you were born, there was no doubt in my mind you had a big heart and an even brighter mind that was meant to cast serenity over this world."

Atlanta could sense every emotion in Lenore's words. She could feel the pain, the ache of a past longed for, one that had once been happy, yet was stripped away. Her heart yearned, as if that same pain had found its way into her soul merely through Lenore's words. She shuddered, and Darian squeezed her hand again. She turned to look at him but he was watching the scene before them, his eyes glistening with unshed tears.

Atlanta looked back at the image of the little boy. There was brightness in his smile, indifference in his bones as he embraced the wind. He looked ready to take on the world, and the world was willing to let him do it.

"I dreamt every single day I would see my Darian blossom and grow. I saw his youth molding him into a man when I closed my eyes."

The bright light shifted as Lenore's gaze moved over to her daughter. "Atlanta, you were born at dawn. A rose that was missing nothing but its thorns. You were more beautiful than I could have ever imagined, and there was nothing in the world I wouldn't have done for you." Lenore's voice shuddered. "I held you both in my arms, and in my heart every morning and at night when dreams took me away."

The scene shifted again. There were roses and daffodils surrounding a house of stone by the sea. In the scene, a five-year-old Darian was throwing stones into the water, watching them skip and then sink. The sound of singing came from inside the house, lullabies in Lenore's voice that were soothing the soft cries of baby Atlanta.

I know those songs.

A sudden melancholy took over. The skies turned a paler shade of purple, and the mountains slept and wept as the stars lay silent in the moon's absence.

The scene shifted again. Atlanta watched as the sea and mountains dwarfed into dark caverns and large bookcases surrounding a round table where many women sat facing each other. Atlanta felt her body shake when her eyes fell on Adelaide, standing at one seat, talking to the audience before her.

"The witches' power stems from the lunar books, and through those they are also controlled. She who can possess all eight possesses all witches and binds them to her will. With power like this, the world as we know it would end." Adelaide stared at the women, her features scrunched in anger, her eyes burning.

Lenore's voice sounded soft against Adelaide's. "The witches knew this, and they were careful not to keep all the books in one place. They knew what power like that could do, the corruption it could bring, the end to what we were made to protect. Adelaide felt otherwise. She wanted all eight books, was determined not to let anything get in her way. She was able to convince a few with the darkest of hearts, promising them immortality and power, a kingdom on earth like no other. They followed her blindly, and destroyed anything in their path. And then they came for me."

The image shifted to darkness, scenes running like parts of a movie, flickering faster than a memory.

"The witches needed an army, and Adelaide knew where to find one. Her desire was to free the hybrids, and for that she needed me, the descendant of the witch who locked up her creations in the first place. They didn't know that the key to opening the door was moved to my daughter once she was born, and so I had to hide you from them. I would take my own life before I let them have yours. I couldn't lose you. I had my brother James take you and flee from Lisbon, back to Calen where you would be safe in the peace that was maintained there."

The feeling of seeing and hearing her mother was alien to her, and so were the emotions that, like purposeless rivers, flowed up and down her spine. Atlanta wanted to believe all that she was hearing. She needed to believe it, because James had lied to her. Why had he kept her mother hidden from her? Until that moment, all her questions about her parents had been unanswered and unaddressed. They were mere shadows within the uncertainty that she lived in day after day.

"And so, I kissed my beloved daughter goodbye and set her sailing across seas to a safety that I was yet unsure of, but I knew that with James I didn't need to worry. I watched over you as you grew, but from afar. When I closed my eyes, I saw the dreams roaming around your mind and absorbing you in."

The scene shifted to a familiar one, one that Atlanta had seen twice before.

"A year after Atlanta left for Calen, Adelaide and the witches arrived, and with them were two of the Lunar Books. One is the book of the half-moon, the one my mother had given herself into and, consequently, I was enslaved to. Adelaide did everything in her power to get me to open the door. Nearly everything. That's when she realized that opening the door was no longer in my power. She was furious. She tortured me and threatened to kill Darian if I didn't tell her where the key was moved."

You died.

Atlanta flinched. It wasn't her thoughts she was hearing, but Darian's.

"I didn't. It was the illusion Adelaide had cast over your eyes, a painful memory that you were to live with for the rest of your life. Adelaide was convinced I didn't know where the power was moved. She sent me to Everlore and bound me to guard the town and the books here. I was compelled to do so, and I've been imprisoned by the walls of this town ever since."

James lied. He never told me. He should've told me.

"Years later, your father led an army of Druids on a campaign to regain control over the book that Adelaide had. He tried to end the misery I was bound to. He managed to defeat Adelaide and her followers, but when Adelaide realized that the book was going to be taken she destroyed it. That left me bound to Everlore. I could never leave it."

"Why not use your magic?" Darian asked. He clearly knew about the Druids' battle. *He lost his father—wait, my father.*

"Yes, I still have the power over myself and the conscious will, but only within the vicinity of the walls of Everlore. I can't leave. I can't fight. I can do nothing but watch you from afar. I watched my husband die. My brother..."

The scenes ended and the light died out. Atlanta felt tears roll down her cheeks, and when she looked to her side she could see Darian crying as well. Their hands were still interlocked.

"My father?" Atlanta stammered.

"He died in his attempts, but not before making sure Darian had a home."

"I was raised by the Druids," Darian whispered, as if answering Atlanta's questions. "I trained amongst them, grew amongst them. Until I became who I am now."

"And what a majestic man you have grown into." Lenore smiled.

Atlanta felt Darian's hand slide out of hers, and she grasped it harder. She turned and met his eyes. "So, I've got a brother? Who happens to be the Coven?" She pretended to roll her eyes. "Figures." Her attention caught on a reflection from the wall. "Are those the other lunar books?" she asked, pointing.

Lenore looked to the wall and nodded. "The books that were in Everlore became mine, and all the witches who were bound by those books were guided into Everlore to follow my rule in this town."

"And you couldn't send for us to help you?" Darian pressed.

"How? I became both powerful and powerless. Never could I see my children again, yet I can move stars and guide the moon's light with the power I was given by these three books."

"And where are the others?" Darian asked.

"I can only assume Adelaide is searching for them. From what I understand, she has one with her now." Lenore sighed, and her eyes shifted from the books to Atlanta. "I have missed you so much, my little rose."

Atlanta's arms vibrated from the intensity of feelings she was experiencing. She was trembling, like a mountain that was about to crumble and fall into the sea. She felt herself weakened by Lenore's words. Tears rolled down her cheeks and she let them flow. There was no stopping the tears that were boiling in her heart since the day she opened her eyes to a motherless world. Seeing her mom after years of not knowing if there was such a thing as a mother's heart in her world made her fingers flow of their own accord, longing to touch her and make sure it was not a trick her mind was playing on her.

She walked forward, almost magnetically towards Lenore. Her mother's head was bowed and her eyes closed. Tears collected in the corners of her eyes and she was trying to keep them in the windows of her soul and hold them back from falling, but they eventually did. When she lifted her head and opened her tear-filled eyes, Atlanta stood close to her, her hand touching hers.

Atlanta took in her mother's face and her figure, trying to fill her memory with the images she should have seen in all the years that had passed.

Lenore held Atlanta in her arms and embraced her. She gestured to Darian, and Atlanta could hear her brother's feet shuffle on the stone floor. "Darian, my son." Lenore's voice trembled. "Come closer."

Atlanta turned and met his gaze, nodding slightly as if she were confirming that he had nothing to fear. His steps were heavy, as if still in disbelief. He clenched his fists and hesitated just out of their reach.

Let go, Darian.

The wind echoed loudly. The howls of it cried in dismay, and the quivering of the land and the trees outside reached the ground under their feet and shook them. There was a series of cries, followed by the red glow of fire from outside.

Darian rushed to the window to look out.

Atlanta let go of Lenore and followed him. Outside, they saw fire on the walls of Everlore, and the echoes of the dying pierced the night.

"What is that?" Darian asked.

"We're under attack," Lenore said from behind them.

Suddenly, the walls shook, and a strong gush of wind burst through the room. Atlanta closed her eyes against the force, and when she opened them there was a new presence in the room. It came accompanied with mocking laughter.

Atlanta crouched, drawing her blade from the back of her suit. From the corner of her eye she could see Darian's fists suddenly burst into fire, his magic returned.

"Am I too late for the family reunion?" Adelaide spread her arms out and threw her head back, laughing.

Chapter 23

"*Careful.*"

Atlanta ignored James' voice, her gaze fixated on Adelaide. From outside came more screaming, and the sounds of ringing bells bellowed with the wind.

Adelaide stood cloaked in bitter black. The strand of her hair that was green spiraled around her like a halo of malice. She had appeared in the watchtower like the passing of a shooting star, suddenly standing in the middle of the room, and the air that accompanied her had taken over the silence that lingered in the spaces between them.

Atlanta's fingers tightened around the handle of her blade, her instincts sharper than her weapon. She briefly glanced at Lenore, who seemed calm, almost as if she'd been expecting Adelaide.

A misty green shone through the windows. Atlanta chanced a quick look over her shoulder and at the scene unfolding outside. The people of Everlore were lined behind the walls, casting green glowing barriers around them, a protection of sorts that stood no chance against the army of hybrids that was breaking through. The roars and screams rang louder. A battle had begun, and the people of Everlore were on the losing side.

"*Stay focused,*" James whispered, and Atlanta spun back around to face the witch. Ravens flew in through the window and perched on the furniture and on Adelaide's shoulders.

Atlanta saw a flickering image of her uncle, standing in a corner, leaning against the wall and watching her intently.

"You've found us, Adelaide," Lenore said, her face giving away nothing.

"You've hidden yourself well, Lenore," Adelaide replied. "Even I, who sent you here, couldn't find my way back into the realm of this town."

"Unlike your hybrids, I have a will that guides me into creating new spells. Ones that will take, even you, centuries to uncover."

"Don't be so sure, Lenore," Adelaide chuckled, her eyes burning bright, her lips drawn into a scowl that sent shivers down Atlanta's spine. "I'll rid you of your power before you can cast another one of your spells."

I'm going to kill her.

"Wait," James' voice echoed in her ear.

But Atlanta was unable to contain the massive surge of anger that was taking over her. She stood facing the woman who'd killed the only man that was close to a father to her. She remembered the look in his eyes as he fell to his knees on the roof. She remembered the ghost of a smile that formed on his face when his eyes met hers before he died.

The image formed in her mind and became clearer, as if she was reliving the moment. A scorching fire was coursing through her veins, burning her from the inside and struggling to get out. It was the blood that was trapped in her clenched fists. They were the tears of rage that were boiling in her eyes.

I'm going to kill her.

Her feet trembled and her legs shook, but in silence. On the inside, her bones were cracking, but on the outside the fierceness was all that showed. The blade in her hand shone as the full moon kissed it from afar. And to her, that was enough of a sign for her to know what she had to do next.

"Don't let your emotions take over," James whispered.

Her body was swayed by a force that was stronger than she had imagined. Fury that was fueled by the images of her uncle kept resonating in her mind. Without a second thought, she shot forward.

"Wait!" James screamed.

Adelaide turned to face her just as the blade found its mark. Atlanta let out a fierce scream and forced the blade in deeper, piercing Adelaide's chest, gazing into the burning green eyes as they burst into flames of rage and fury.

Adelaide reached for her but Atlanta was quick, pulling the blade back and then striking again. "That one's for my uncle."

Adelaide dropped to her knees, clutching her chest.

"The other one's for my mother," Atlanta spat, glancing up to look at Lenore. She hesitated at the look on Lenore's face. Shock... and fear. Atlanta frowned, unable to understand why, riding high on the adrenaline that coursed through her and the feeling of victory that washed over her.

Adelaide's hands fell to the floor and drops of green blood spread around them. Atlanta seized the moment of weakness and dug her sword into Adelaide's back, leaving the blade there. Adelaide screamed once and then sank into silence as more and more of her blood began pooling around her hands.

"It's over, Adelaide." Atlanta glared at the witch and then froze.

Something was wrong.

The witch's body was shaking, and low, guttural laughter could barely be heard over the thundering roars of the battles outside. The laughter grew louder, and Adelaide's body began to fade. Like dust being blown off a surface, her body turned to ashes as her manic laughter echoed against the walls around them.

Within seconds, Adelaide's body disappeared and only the blade remained.

"It's over, right?" Atlanta gasped, looking over at Darian. She flinched as, outside, the screaming continued and the sounds of fire flickering and wood crackling masked her victory.

"You mistake Adelaide's malice," Lenore said, rushing to the Luna Books on the wall and tearing them down from their bindings.

"You saw that, didn't you?" Atlanta asked in disbelief. "I killed her. She's dead. Gone. Disappeared. Darian?"

Darian opened his mouth to answer, but Lenore pushed the books into his hands. "She's not dead," she said. "If Adelaide falls, so do her hybrids." She pointed to the window. "But the beasts are still fighting."

"Then there's got to be another explanation," Atlanta stammered.

"There is none!" Lenore snapped, her eyes darting through the room. "Quick now, you must leave."

She was pushing them both forward when a burst of green light exploded behind them. Atlanta turned just in time to see Adelaide appear in the flames, her laughter shaking the walls around them. Lenore turned, and her hands burst into flames of blue as she stood between them and the witch.

"Just as naïve as her mother!" Adelaide mocked.

"Go!" Lenore yelled, and with a swift movement of her hands she threw up a wall of blue flames just as green fire shot towards them. The collision of power blinded Atlanta, and she shielded her eyes against the sudden light. She felt a hand grab her arm and pull, and she fought against it.

"Let me go!" she yelled, grabbing for her sword.

"Atlanta, no!" Darian shouted, his grip tightening on her arm.

She turned and shot him an angry look, her lips pulled back in a snarl, her eyes threatening. A second collision of magic threw her off her feet, and she slammed into Darian, sending them both sprawling out the door. She jumped to her feet, ready to race back inside, when the door slammed shut.

"Darian, help me!" she screamed, throwing her body against the door. It wouldn't open, and she began kicking at it frantically. Light from inside burst around the sides of the door, the battle between Lenore and Adelaide hidden from her sight. Atlanta screamed as she continued her attack.

"Atlanta!" Darian grabbed her by the arm and forcefully turned her around. She was crying now, and if she hadn't been able to control herself she would've struck him with her blade.

"We need to go," he stated firmly. "She wants us to leave. We have to protect the Lunar Books."

"I'm not leaving her!" Atlanta shot back. "I'm not losing her! Not now!"

"She can take care of herself!" Darian yelled. "Let's go, or all this will be for nothing. Now!"

Atlanta looked back at the door and the flashes of light bursting from under the threshold. She hesitated, wanting to ignore Darian and try to get back inside to fight.

He's right.

She cursed and, with a second glance at the door, nodded and followed Darian down the stairs.

Chapter 24

Everlore lay in turmoil.

It was burning.

Dying.

Fighting with its last breath.

The second Atlanta and Darian set foot outside the watchtower, flames lapped at their skin and the fumes made them gag. Explosions resounded all around them, mixed with the screams of the dying and the victorious hissing of the hybrids. Everywhere they looked, there was death and destruction.

"The city's falling," Darian yelled over the sound of the flames and screams.

Atlanta nodded, quickly glancing back up at the watchtower before returning her attention to the task at hand. "How do we get out of here?"

"This way." Darian grabbed her arm and pulled her along.

They ran through the streets of Everlore, darting between shadows, avoiding the flames, barely making it past falling houses and bleeding corpses. Atlanta could only imagine what Calen had looked like when the hybrids had first escaped, and she knew beyond a doubt that the people of Everlore were facing a similar fate.

As they sprinted, all Atlanta could think about was her mother back in the watchtower with Adelaide, fighting a battle that could go either way. She hoped Lenore would emerge victorious, but a part of her believed that she had seen her mother for the last time. *The first and last time.* A surge of emotions raced through her, and she channeled her rage into her need to get out of Everlore.

Darian's magic restored, they raced through the remains of the city with his magic shielding them, holding off friend and foe alike, cloaking them when needed, and burning through the enemy when required. She did her best to keep up, knowing that if it were not for the Lunar Books they would probably make better progress.

They rounded a corner, and the crumbled remains of Everlore's outer walls came into view. There was little standing between them and freedom, the bulk of the battle having moved towards the center of the town and around the watchtower.

If the hybrids reach the watchtower, Lenore has no chance.

The thought blinded Atlanta, and for a brief second made her hesitate and stop.

Darian turned to her. "What's wrong?" he asked. "Come on, we're almost there."

"I can't," Atlanta whispered.

Darian rushed to her and pulled her along. "Not the time or place," he hissed. "We'll be back for her later."

"I just found her. I can't leave her behind."

Darian's expression turned to rage. "You think I'm happy about this?" he spat. "You think I'm okay with leaving her behind with that witch, again? When this time I could actually be of some use?"

"Darian–"

"These are what's important!" Darian yelled, holding the books up for her to see. "They're more important than Lenore. More important than Raul, who I fear may be dead already. These are what stands between Adelaide and the end of the world as we know it. And despite every emotion racing through me, despite everything I feel, I know there's nothing I can do other than my duty. I'm the leader of the

Coven, and you're the last warrior of Calen. Our duties come before anything else!"

Tears stung her eyes. She returned her brother's firm gaze, a part of her still wanting to protest, to tell him that he was wrong, that family was the most important thing in the world. Only, she couldn't. *Because he's right.*

"Now, let's go before we won't be able to," Darian said.

"Hurry, hurry," a low, familiar voice hissed from between the flames. "Why in such a hurry?"

Atlanta recognized the voice immediately, unsheathing her blade just as Darian's hands burst into flames. From between the flames of the adjacent house a figure walked out, slowly and confidently, fangs glistening in the dim light, eyes burning red.

"You should never leave a party without saying goodbye." Michael sniggered, stepping out of the flames and standing between them and the remains of Everlore's walls.

Atlanta stepped forward, her hands tightened around the hilt of her long blade. "Come to pick a fight?"

The hybrid laughed. "Come to join your uncle?"

Atlanta was about to take a step forward when Darian stopped her. "Out of our way, monster."

"You have no power over me, Druid." Michael moved to step around him toward Atlanta.

"No," Darian replied, "but I can burn you to the ground right here."

Michael cocked his head to one side and his red eyes burned brighter. "Not if I get you first," he mocked. "It'll be fun tormenting Atlanta by killing another of her flesh and blood while she watches helplessly."

"No!" Atlanta raised her sword.

"It's a trick." Darian looked at her. "We don't have time for this. He's trying to stall us."

"He's not as weak as you think," Atlanta said to Michael, ignoring Darian. "We have unfinished business."

Darian took a step back and let the fire in his hands die.

Michael burst into laughter. "Adelaide has no more use for you," he hissed. "I promise not to laugh when I rip your head from your shoulders."

"Let's see if you bleed green," Atlanta shot back.

Michael snapped at her, and with a deep growl launched himself towards her. Atlanta pushed Darian to the side and rolled out of the hybrid's way, but Michael was quicker. He turned almost immediately, grabbing Atlanta by the leg and swinging her to the side.

She crashed to the ground, her sword flying from her hand. She pushed to her feet, watching as Darian shot green flames at Michael, only for the hybrid to dodge the attack and come for her again. From behind a building, two more hybrids appeared. Darian turned to stop them.

Atlanta rolled again, dodging Michael's attack, but this time drawing her short daggers from her suit and throwing them at him. The daggers sliced through empty air, and she felt her breath suddenly knocked out of her as the hybrid slammed into her and threw her back. She landed with a thud, her head spinning.

She tried to kick him off, but he lifted her shoulders and threw her hard into the cobblestones below them. Her head hit the ground and the world suddenly darkened.

She lost consciousness, falling into an abyss of nothingness.

* * *

"*I warned you.*"

Atlanta couldn't see her uncle, but James' voice was clear in the darkness around her.

"*I told you your emotions would be your undoing.*"

"I had her," Atlanta whispered. "I felt my blade slice through her."

"There's still so much to learn," James replied. *"And I can't be there to teach you. You'll have to start making wiser decisions. Decisions you were accustomed to me making for you."*

Atlanta felt a shudder race through her. A sudden realization dawned on her. "I won't make it through this, will I?"

"You will," James said. *"But to do it, you must find peace. You must find acceptance. You must find yourself."*

"I'm lost."

"No, you only believe you are," James replied. *"But look how far you've come. You've found your mother, learned about your past, understood where you fit in this world. You're not just the defender of Calen anymore. You defend everyone."*

"It's too much," Atlanta sobbed. "I can't do this alone."

"You're not alone," James replied. *"You have Darian. You have Ryan. You have the races of Vampires and Werewolves at your disposal. They'll follow you, if you lead. And you can't lead if you don't forgive yourself."*

"But all of this," Atlanta stammered. "I did this. I caused this. You're dead because of me."

"No one decides their fate. I died protecting what I loved, as will you one day. But that day hasn't come yet. Forgive yourself, Atlanta. Forgive yourself."

Atlanta opened her mouth to reply, when a sudden burst of pain erupted inside her and her throat clenched. And with that, the darkness subsided.

* * *

"You're mine," Michael hissed.

Atlanta's eyes fluttered open. Michael held her by the neck, high above the ground. She violently tried kicking her legs in the air to break free of his hold. Darian was still fighting one of the other hybrids; his green fire had knocked one down, the other he was now tossing about like a rag doll. And yet they kept getting up and attacking him. She knew he couldn't keep it up much longer.

"Say hello to your uncle for me, child," Michael chuckled.

Forgive yourself.

Atlanta closed her eyes and let her emotions wash over her. In her mind, she saw her past, a kaleidoscope of images of her life with James—training, laughing, crying. She saw Ryan smiling at her, his eyes saying so much without the need for words. She saw Calen, the beauty of the city, the dark corners that promised malice but shimmered with life and peace. She saw everyone and everything she loved, wrapped up in a sheath of warmth, held together, drawn to her, guiding her. And she saw Darian fighting by her side, holding her hand, promising a new life, fighting together.

And through it all, she saw Lenore. She heard the lullabies. And she saw the truth.

She was the last wall between this world and the world of monsters. She was the master, the Coven Master meant to the keep of peace. She was a Druid, a warrior of the Coven, salvation and punishment all in one. And if she had been used to set the hybrids free, it was her duty to rid the world of them. Of Adelaide.

She was not to be blamed for the evil in the world.

But she could be blamed for failing to fight.

She opened her eyes, and for the first time since she had laid eyes on the hybrid Michael's expression changed from his usual cocky confidence to one of fear. Atlanta felt her eyes burning, and the fire in her mind spreading through her veins. She grew stronger, more in tune with herself—something that had lain dormant in her broke free.

"Impossible," Michael whispered.

She grabbed the hand around her neck and pulled it away, dropping silently to the ground. She stood and blocked each swing he took at her. Reaching between his arms, she wrapped her hand around his neck and squeezed with all her might. She felt different. Stronger.

Michael gagged, trying to break free of her hold, but she wouldn't let him go.

"You can't have magic," he gasped as he struggled against her. "It's impossible."

"You're done," she whispered, realizing she was hovering in the air holding him away from her. "This is the end for you."

"A-Adelaide will avenge m-me," Michael stammered, his fangs snapping at her, his eyes burning red.

"I'm counting on it." And with that, she let the magic loose. It rushed out of her in waves, as if a dam had been broken and a flood let loose. It shot up her arm, red fire burning, and engulfed Michael completely.

The hybrid screamed, fighting to break loose, but still she held him. And with a final push of force, he exploded into ashes in her hand.

The other hybrids stopped their attack, confused by this sudden surge of power. She turned to them, and smiled when they raced toward her. Before they could reach her, she rushed to her blade, grabbed it, and sliced through them with the same red fire that had enveloped Michael. The hybrids burst into ash.

Atlanta lowered her weapon and turned towards Darian, his eyes wide and his mouth open.

"It's time to leave," she said. Without waiting for a response, she turned and raced past the broken walls of Everlore.

Epilogue

"You failed me." Adelaide sat in the large chair facing the window of the watchtower, watching Everlore burn. Behind her knelt three of her hybrids.

"My queen, she overpowered the First," one of the hybrids hissed.

Adelaide's face shifted into a deep scowl, her eyes burning a bright green. The death of her favorite hybrid sent waves of rage coursing through her. All she could think of was finding Atlanta Skolar and burning her alive.

"The books are gone?"

The hybrids didn't reply. Adelaide stood up in anger, tossing the chair aside. A bright flash of green escaped her fingers and one of the hybrids exploded into a cloud of dust. The other two flinched, but were smart enough to keep their positions.

"The books are gone!" Adelaide screamed, her voice shaking the walls.

"Yes, my queen," one of the hybrids replied.

"Where is she now?" Adelaide demanded.

"Our scouts saw her leave towards Calen," came the low reply. "We believe she aims to rejoin what remains of the rebellion there."

"But do not fear, my queen," the other hybrid quickly cut in. "Her efforts will prove fruitless. The remaining Wolves and Vampires are scattered. We heard Marcus himself is on the run. She returns to a city with no hope."

"Fools," Adelaide spat. "She has the books. That will be enough to give her hope. I want her stopped before she gets to the city."

"Yes, my queen," the hybrids said in unison.

Adelaide turned back to face the flames of Everlore. Soon it would look the way it had when she'd first brought Lenore here: broken, desolate, without hope or life. A dark place for the darkest of creatures. And they would all bow to her command.

"And what about the woman?"

Adelaide turned, shifting her gaze to where the hybrids were looking. The lifeless body of Lenore lay sprawled on the floor, her blue eyes staring into nothing. Adelaide smiled. "Place her head on a stake at the top of this watchtower." Adelaide scoffed, thinking of the child returning to find her mother. "Burn the rest."

The hybrids nodded, quickly gathering Lenore's body and slithering out of the room before Adelaide's mood changed.

She watched them leave, then turned back to the window and gazed out at the flames. In the fire she saw the future, and how the rest of the world would burn in her wake. The Lunar Books would be hers, and then the entire world would be hers to rule.

But first she needed to destroy the last of Beatrice's line, once and for all.

"I will see you again, Atlanta Skolar," she promised the wind. "And when I do, I promise to be slow and merciless." Her laughter shook the watchtower and soared high over the sounds of the burning city below.

THE END

Alpha's Permission Blurb

Paranormal Huntress Series

Never Look Back
Coven Master
Alpha's Permission

Find W.J. May

Website:
http://www.wanitamay.yolasite.com
Facebook:
https://www.facebook.com/pages/Author-WJ-May-FAN-PAGE/
141170442608149
Newsletter:
SIGN UP FOR W.J. May's Newsletter to find out about new releases,
updates, cover reveals and even freebies!
http://eepurl.com/97aYf

More books by W.J. May

The Chronicles of Kerrigan

Book I - *Rae of Hope* is FREE!
Book Trailer:
http://www.youtube.com/watch?v=gILAwXxx8MU
Book II - *Dark Nebula*
Book Trailer:
http://www.youtube.com/watch?v=Ca24STi_bFM

PREQUEL –
Christmas Before the Magic

SEQUEL –
Matter of Time

Hidden Secrets Saga:
Download Seventh Mark For FREE

Like most teenagers, Rouge is trying to figure out who she is and what she wants to be. With little knowledge about her past, she has questions but has never tried to find the answers. Everything changes when she befriends a strangely intoxicating family. Siblings Grace and Michael, appear to have secrets which seem connected to Rouge. Her hunch is confirmed when a horrible incident occurs at an outdoor party. Rouge may be the only one who can find the answer.

An ancient journal, a Sioghra necklace and a special mark force life-altering decisions for a girl who grew up unprepared to fight for her life or others.

All secrets have a cost and Rouge's determination to find the truth can only lead to trouble...or something even more sinister.

RADIUM HALOS - THE SENSELESS SERIES

Book 1 is FREE:

Everyone needs to be a hero at one point in their life.

The small town of Elliot Lake will never be the same again.

Caught in a sudden thunderstorm, Zoe, a high school senior from Elliot Lake, and five of her friends take shelter in an abandoned uranium mine. Over the next few days, Zoe's hearing sharpens drastically, beyond what any normal human being can detect. She tells her friends, only to learn that four others have an increased sense as well. Only Kieran, the new boy from Scotland, isn't affected.

Fashioning themselves into superheroes, the group tries to stop the strange occurrences happening in their little town. Muggings, break-ins, disappearances, and murder begin to hit too close to home. It leads the team to think someone knows about their secret - someone who wants them all dead.

An incredulous group of heroes. A traitor in the midst. Some dreams are written in blood.

Courage Runs Red

The Blood Red Series

Book 1 is FREE

What if courage was your only option?

When Kallie lands a college interview with the city's new hot-shot police officer, she has no idea everything in her life is about to change. The detective is young, handsome and seems to have an unnatural ability to stop the increasing local crime rate. Detective Liam's particular interest in Kallie sends her heart and head stumbling over each other.

When a raging blood feud between vampires spills into her home, Kallie gets caught in the middle. Torn between love and family loyalty she must find the courage to fight what she fears the most and possibly risk everything, even if it means dying for those she loves.

Daughter of Darkness
Victoria
Only Death Could Stop Her Now
The Daughters of Darkness is a series of female heroines who may or
may not know each other, but all have the same father, Vlad Montour.
Victoria is a Hunter Vampire

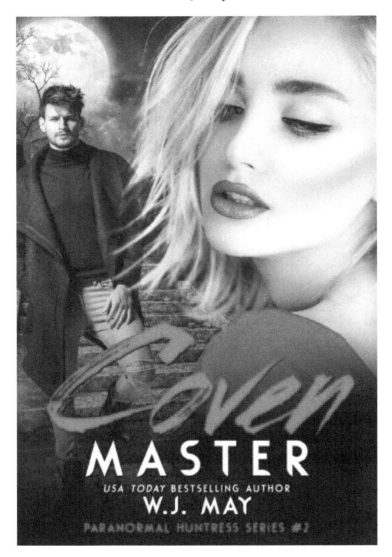

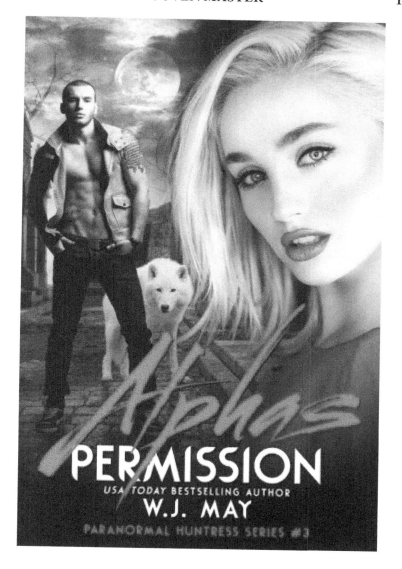

Don't miss out!

Click the button below and you can sign up to receive emails whenever W.J. May publishes a new book. There's no charge and no obligation.

https://books2read.com/r/B-A-SSF-LOXN

Connecting independent readers to independent writers.

Did you love *Coven Master*? Then you should read *Only the Beginning* by W.J. May!

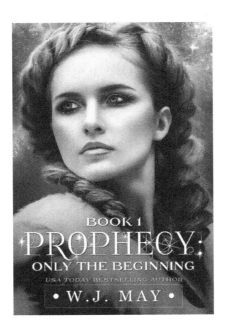

USA TODAY Bestselling author, W.J. May brings you the highly antici-pated continuation of the Hidden Secrets Saga. The Twisted Red Riding Hood fairytale continues in the Prophecy Series. This is a stand alone se-ries, or maybe be read in continuation of the Seventh Mark books.

Be Prepared. There are werewolves in this story, and they are NOT friendly.

Peace comes at a price...

Rebekah and Jamie are happy, but discontent. Sometimes, it feels like everything important has already happened, that the peace their parents fought so hard to bring them is just a strange limbo they can't break out of. They want adventure, they want to make memories of their own. When a pair of new kids show up at their school, it looks like they might finally have their chance.

It isn't long before the twins open up to the mysterious new strangers. Sharing secrets they thought they'd never tell. Asking questions they never could have imagined.

When a party in the woods leads to near tragedy, they find themselves caught in the middle of a fight they never saw coming. Trapped between two sides and put to the ultimate test.

Will they choose their family? Or their future?

Rogue's adventure may have come to an end, but the twins is just getting started...

PROPHECY SERIES
In the Beginning
White Winter
Secrets of Destiny
HIDDEN SECRETS SAGA
Seventh Mark - Part 1
Seventh Mark - Part 2
Marked by Destiny
Compelled
Fate's Intervention
Chosen Three

Also by W.J. May

Bit-Lit Series
Lost Vampire
Cost of Blood
Price of Death

Blood Red Series
Courage Runs Red
The Night Watch
Marked by Courage
Forever Night

Daughters of Darkness: Victoria's Journey
Victoria
Huntress
Coveted (A Vampire & Paranormal Romance)
Twisted

Hidden Secrets Saga

Seventh Mark - Part 1
Seventh Mark - Part 2
Marked By Destiny
Compelled
Fate's Intervention
Chosen Three
The Hidden Secrets Saga: The Complete Series

Paranormal Huntress Series
Never Look Back
Coven Master

Prophecy Series
Only the Beginning
White Winter
Secrets of Destiny

The Chronicles of Kerrigan
Rae of Hope
Dark Nebula
House of Cards
Royal Tea
Under Fire
End in Sight
Hidden Darkness
Twisted Together
Mark of Fate
Strength & Power

Last One Standing
Rae of Light
The Chronicles of Kerrigan Box Set Books # 1 - 6

The Chronicles of Kerrigan: Gabriel
Living in the Past
Present For Today

The Chronicles of Kerrigan Prequel
Christmas Before the Magic
Question the Darkness
Into the Darkness
Fight the Darkness
Alone in the Darkness
Lost in Darkness
The Chronicles of Kerrigan Prequel Series Books #1-3

The Chronicles of Kerrigan Sequel
A Matter of Time
Time Piece
Second Chance
Glitch in Time
Our Time
Precious Time

The Hidden Secrets Saga

Seventh Mark (part 1 & 2)

The Senseless Series
Radium Halos
Radium Halos - Part 2
Nonsense

Standalone
Shadow of Doubt (Part 1 & 2)
Five Shades of Fantasy
Shadow of Doubt - Part 2
Four and a Half Shades of Fantasy
Dream Fighter
What Creeps in the Night
Forest of the Forbidden
HuNted
Arcane Forest: A Fantasy Anthology
Ancient Blood of the Vampire and Werewolf

Made in the USA
Las Vegas, NV
04 March 2021